ADVANCE PRAISE
THE REMNANT.

"Hill's characters are so precisely written, they feel as real as you and me, despite the generations of inbreeding, which have left them somewhere off the 'normal' scale. Yet, these folks love and hope and yearn like the rest of us, and their stories are magical. Hill has the silver tongue of a master wordsmith. His gorgeous prose rambles from hilarious to sly to clever, and then doubles back so it can dive right off into beautiful, heartsick, and poignant. A standout story with unbelievably effective prose, *The Remnants* is one of my favorite 2016 titles."
— Dianah Hughley, bookseller, Powell's City of Books

"Nobody wants to be compared to James Joyce. Especially, I'd imagine, Robert Hill. So I won't. But in Hill's novel, *The Remnants*, like Leopold Bloom, Kennesaw Belvedere wakes up one fine morning and goes forth into his beloved city. Along his way, worlds open up into worlds, stories beget stories beget stories, and characters live and breathe and die of just about every ailment in the almanac. Really you wonder how you can go on with all the living and the breathing and the dying, but Hill's language is such a thing of rare beauty that you love every moment. And when Hunko finds Kennesaw, and Molly and Leopold are yes, of all the brilliant moments in the novel, there's one final brilliant moment, one perfectly still moment, when all is well in a decaying world. If you love language and if you love narrative and if you love stories, don't pass up *The Remnants*."
— Tom Spanbauer, author of
The Man Who Fell in Love with the Moon

"Bold, brilliant, and touching, *The Remnants* is a eulogy for a world in which humanity is treasured—a celebration of life in all its imperfect glory."
— Rene Denfeld, author of *The Enchanted*

"Wholly unexpected and unique, Hill fills his bewitching telling of the last days of a small town and its few remaining genetically compromised residents with wordplay that belies the power of connection, memory, and community."
— Elisa Saphier, lead bookseller, Another Read Through

"As to the meaning of this novel, with its sentences coiling around themselves like a celtic knot, I think it comes down to this: it's a book about that most primal of urges, the urge to procreate. In *The Remnants* that urge runs amuck. It defies the boundaries humans have placed upon it in order that the species might not turn in upon itself. That urge carries with it the desire for connection, for a bond with another human, the two urges inextricably wound around each other, and in New Eden the possibilities are so limited that the distinctions between one family and the next have all but disappeared. The genetic results are of course calamitous, and the emotional consequences are littered across the novel's landscape. To turn too far inward, the novel tells us, is to invite disaster."
 – Stevan Allred, author of *A Simplified Map of the Real World*

"Such extravagant, rambunctious delicious language! And a sad and wonderful story of the end of the town of New Eden and its inbred and lyrical inhabitants. I have never read a book like this before. It defies genre."
 – Cindy Heidemann, field sales, Legato Publishers Group

PRAISE FOR ROBERT HILL'S DEBUT NOVEL
WHEN ALL IS SAID AND DONE
(GRAYWOLF PRESS, 2006)

"Every aspect of this agile, intoxicating, hilarious, and poignant novel is compelling, but what elevates it is the exuberant language. Hill writes with velocity, rhythm, and wit, conveying a world of subtle emotions and social nuance in brilliantly syncopated inner monologues and staccato dialogue, creating a bravura and resounding performance."
 – Donna Seaman, *Booklist*

"With evocative, freewheeling prose ('the run-on sentences that were her married life'), Hill . . . nimbly salvages one family's striving from an era of grasping and consumerism."
 – *Publishers Weekly*

"Truly the most enjoyable, evocative prose I've come across in new fiction in quite a while."
 – *City Pages*

"*When All Is Said and Done* is a fresh, high-velocity cry from the heart, showing that love is the rose and the thorn at once, and that Mr. Robert Hill has taken a running start into what they used to call the literary scene."
— Ron Carlson, author of *A Kind of Flying*

"This is a witty, generous, heartbreaking book which seeks . . . 'the common green in our beings'—and finds it."
— Barbara McMichael, *The Olympian*

"In flitting seamlessly from the mundane details of daily life to broader questions of love, family, priorities, and death, the author has created a startlingly realistic depiction of the way the mind functions."
— *Kirkus Reviews*

"Hill's novel is strong for all that it does say, and all that it leaves to the reader's imagination. There's something poetic in the best of ways about the way that the lines and language unfold. This book reminds me of Cheever and Yates and a young Rick Moody."
— A.M. Homes, author of *May We Be Forgiven*

"Lively and quirky and effervescent with beautiful, unpredictable language and fresh details. A novel of an incredible vitality, original and vibrating, of a superb unforeseeable and detailed writing to the extreme."
— Edmund White, author of *A Boy's Own Story*

"Not many writers will risk burying a gem like 'memory is such a sloppy librarian' in the middle of a paragraph. Not so Robert Hill. In his lovely first book . . . there's hardly a neutral sentence in sight."
— Nell Beram, *Harvard Review*

"From the first glorious sentence to the last astounding word, Robert Hill's *When All Is Said and Done* is a treasure. The sophisticated wit and luxurious language of this brilliant novel weave a story of one family's complex heart and history and their journey through 1950s/60s suburban Connecticut and all its prejudices. Read this American saga and weep."
— Tom Spanbauer, author of *I Loved You More*

"Out of nowhere comes Robert Hill's *When All Is Said and Done*, a swift, moving novel of the 1950s from a man who has been writing advertising copy in Portland, Oregon, for twenty years. Its form resembles the alternate first-person accounts of a troubled relationship in Julian Barnes's *Talking It Over*; in its historical shimmer, it recalls Richard Yates's increasingly beloved *Revolutionary Road*. . . . Reading Mr. Hill's debut novel reminds us how usual most novels are; his is unusual, but not unsettling or obviously weird. Perhaps it is simply the work of an individual who has been minding his own business in Portland."

– Benjamin Lytal, *The New York Sun*

"His is the sort of book which you find yourself wanting to write down passages of particular grace—only to realize that alone, they appear unremarkable. It's in context of this affecting book that each scene is so striking. . . . Above all, it's a love story, one complicated with careers and children and growth and stagnancy: completely mundane and completely extraordinary."

– Molly Templeton, *Eugene Weekly*

"A snappy, palatable iteration of modernism, too earnest and heartfelt to be called postanything."

– Patrick Somerville, *Bookshop Bibliosurf*

"Exuberant as a rhythmic song, the first novel by Robert Hill is not only smart, it is brilliant, stylish, and offers not a novel but a dramatic existential novel."

– Jean Soublin, *Le Monde*

"Simultaneously prosaic and breathtaking, *All's Well That Ends* (French translation) is the first novel of a great writer in the tradition of Raymond Carver."

– Payot & Rivages

THE REMNANTS

THE REMNANTS

ROBERT HILL

FOREST AVENUE PRESS
Portland, Oregon

Library of Congress Cataloging-in-Publication Data
Names: Hill, Robert (Robert Scott), 1959- author.
Title: The remnants / by Robert Hill.
Description: Portland, OR : Forest Avenue Press, [2016]
Identifiers: LCCN 2015040169 | ISBN 9781942436157 (pbk.)
Classification: LCC PS3608.I4376 R46 2016 | DDC 813/.6--dc23LC
record available at http://lccn.loc.gov/2015040169

ISBN: 978-1-942436-15-7

1 2 3 4 5 6 7 8 9

Distributed by Legato Publishers Group

Printed in the United States of America
by Forest Avenue Press LLC
Portland, Oregon

Cover design: Gigi Little
Moss image: Roberto Verzo
Interior design: Laura Stanfill
Publicist: Mary Bisbee-Beek

Forest Avenue Press LLC
6327 SW Capitol Highway, Suite C
PMB 218
Portland, OR 97239
forestavenuepress.com

For
R.B. & Mr. B.,
eternally

Heavily hangs the broad sunflower
Over its grave i' the earth so chilly;
Heavily hangs the hollyhock,
Heavily hangs the tiger-lily.

– "A Spirit Haunts the Year's Last Hours"
by Alfred, Lord Tennyson

1. TRUE

AS TRUE BLISS LAY in her bed on the morning of the eve of her one hundredth birthday, the thought that circled her mind, in the applesauce eddy of her mind, the first chunk in the applesauce eddy that her mind could sink its teeth into was please don't let this day be my last day on earth. She had not slept well in the night, nor had she slept well on the one before this, and worse was her sleep on the one before that. It had been too long since she could remember nights of sleeping well, or sleeping some or sleeping at all, and last night's not sleeping well was a subject she couldn't put to rest, and it lay in her ample bed with her and took up space along with her hopes of another day. It was the last clear thought she was to entertain.

She drowsed in that bed that was more bed than she'd needed for years, the bed that grew larger over the years as her already small self lost its roundness and tautness and collapsed into a pool of slack skin that had no will of its own. She had long ago gotten used to the affront of nature taking back from her the size it had only loaned, but to lie in a bed that seemed to grow in its mockery of her predicament as she withered and diminished was downright small-minded. Petty for petty, she wished this waking nightmare on only those most like her. She spit up a little apple seed of a laugh at the thought, for ever since she could remember she had once or twice a week wished it on all three of the Lope triplets, those diminutive demon spawns born in the winter of the year of no summer, whose lungs could suck a day of its life and whose nocturnal screams from infancy on up had deprived the whole town of truly deep sleep since they were pushed up from hell all those years ago. Even long after the passings of Onesie Lope and Twosie Lope in their sixty-seventh and seventy-ninth years respectively, True harbored feelings of ill will and worse sleep on their surviving sibling, Threesie, True's favorite if she had to choose, for it was Threesie's screams most searing of all that pierced eardrums and shattered canning jars throughout the valley and on some nights could make a full moon run for cover. Even though the earth swallowed Threesie's lone screams some years ago, to True their echo is a living thing strong enough to make a night of it still. She stared from the coddled milk pools of her eyes at the fading night sky above her bed that so reminded her of the paint-flecked ceiling of her bedroom, and if she could only have ten pure minutes, minutes free of Threesie's screams, ten minutes of uninterrupted, mindless, wakeless night, she'd let her heart wander through a century of days and run it to pasture like so many sheep.

LORE HAS IT THAT back when New Eden was to apples as its namesake was to hanky-panky, every family for sixty-nine square miles was as cross-pollinated as the town's prized Granny-Macs. True Bliss's mother, her name was Cozy, and her father, his name was Remedial, the last of the Remedials, were second cousins from two withering branches of the Bliss family tree; kin whose brief, and to all accounts, indifferent acquaintance prior to marriage never really warmed above freezing. Family and town lore has it, it took six long winters and one slow-to-start spring before Cozy and Remedial Bliss did what married cousins do in private. Everyone in New Eden was good about keeping their hush up when it came to the indifferent relations in the Bliss house, the big white house with the twelve prized apple trees all in a row, True's house. But come spring in its entirety, when the first of the blossoms on the apple trees beyond the barn began to show and Cozy did, too, there wasn't a set of eleven fingers in town that couldn't count to six and a half years without pointing and laughing.

Neighbor ladies clucked as neighbor ladies will, sitting on the front porch with Cozy as she swelled through the summer and into the high corn. Down river a drop, out on the bank back of the New Eden Grangery, chuckles and snorts breezed with the blackflies as the menfolk blinked daylight over a passing jug of hard cider, nattering their own buzz about Remedial and his best friend Bull Engersol. Nothing that Remedial ever started was ever finished without Bull's help, and there were sniggers galore that that went as much for husbanding as hoeing. Between generous swigs and hearty knee-slaps, their neck fat quivering like virgins, they'd say, *Sumpin' got remedial with Cozy, but it wudn't Remedial. You ask me, Bull rode that cow to calf.*

August stretched as far as the eye can see and then some, the apples on the trees beyond the barn grew fat and arrogant, and lore will out that it was ten days into September, a Sabbath date, that Remedial Bliss took his jug and some foolishness out to Grunts Pond and likely drowned there. Cozy's confinement began to near its end on that very same afternoon and with the moon fully dunked in all that heavenly blackness she gave birth the following dawn to the cousins' only child, grafted like their prized trees to standard rootstock and grown true, the daughter she named without spit from her husband. Grafting and widowhood agreed with Cozy. She wanted her daughter's name to reflect that. So she named her True. True Bliss.

IN HER LIFETIME TRUE had skipped to her Lou with sparklers in a sulfur haze and danced a maypole with boots laced high. She tended fevers and blisters and wounds and welts, she drank her applejack neat and ate her chervil raw, and as a girl with no concern for womanhood beyond her youth, saw relations of any amorous kind as nothing more than pennies and pins in a drawer full of nonsense. In dust heaps and scrap piles and corncribs, she trembled for mankind and her own kind over the terrible natures that the unkind unleash. She knew her multiplication tables before she learned the difference between boys and girls and what it could add up to. She could spin a cartwheel like no one's business. She could fart a skunk. With her eyes closed she could hoe a row straight to an eighth of an inch, she could clean a gun, she could bone a fish, she could thread cornsilk through a bent needle's eye. For as many years as she has been mistress of her own home, which is more than even she can remember, she has kept the Good Book in her front parlor; it makes a righteous doorstop. True hated her absent father, but in time forgave him his trespasses. In time she came to hate her mother more, and begrudged her her trespasses for all eternity for sending away the only boy True might have loved. Only nature earns True's glory, and to her the only thing worthy of psalms is the sound September makes when autumn breezes the trees.

Two things known in this world are two rounds of ammunition you don't want aimed at her for fear of retribution: one is jack-in-the-pulpits and the other is pink velvet ribbons.

True was the firstborn of the last of us all, and at last, the eldest elder we had; she was the elder every younger has always looked to for guidance. She slowed a bit in her sixties as the world sped upward, and ached in her seventies as it moved onward and away, she rusted in her eighties as it moved past her and beyond, and although she never could curse worth a darn, she bitched and pained and moaned and mourned through the seeming endlessness of her nineties till now, and here she is on the cusp of a suddenly-too-soon-century wanting to mark the occasion with the dawn of one more day. Beyond this, she'll stop herself from thinking. She has one more night ahead in which to not sleep well, and all of eternity to catch up. Well she knows that for all its length and furor, life is as brief as a breath when compared to forever.

2: KENNESAW

DOWN A MORNING'S WALK from True's house where
the town's main road runs out of itself, two slip-sloped
ruts take over on the way to a buckled-up foursquare
where one more day is one more day is one more day
too many.

Kennesaw Belvedere is of the mind that what you
put into a day isn't always what you get out of it, and
after a while, often after too long a lived while, you wish
to hell you could just get out of it.

This life.

Even skin and bones like he is needs oats shoveled
in on a regular basis to get the tide flowing, oats and

greens and a nip of what-ails-ya. But when this true and tried method fails to move the boats out into the bay, a skin and bones man can be one stopped-up sumbitch, stopped up like he is today, like he was yesterday, like he's been all week—a man on the can with a plugged canal, that's Kennesaw.

Kennesaw Buckett Belvedere.

What he puts into his day isn't always what he gets out.

Ordinarily, the man is all bluer-than-blue eyes and cleft and chisel, and no matter what else looks good on him, those eyes alone carry the day. Those bluer-than-blues are what the skies copy for color, and when they take their time to blink, your heart stops until they come back open again. Kennesaw has made a lifetime of his blues. They've done his bidding; they get him tomatoes out of season, they get his overalls ironed, they get him firewood stacked cord upon cord. Jubilee Aspetuck once swallowed a pin when those eyes bored holes in her for hemming a leg too high. And Hunko Minton, he'd have no reason to ever wake again if those eyes were to shut for good. Those eyes, the bluest corn blue of them, when you see them, they move you, they move mountains, they make glaciers want to carve clean streams. Those bluer-than-blues ascended Kennesaw above the ordinary and floated him supernatural; all his life has been a levitation beyond mere mortality and the grounding odors of the everyday. But dammed shut by force of a clogged bowel push, shut like they are now on the man, the man on the can with his overalls down around his ankles who's pushing and pushing and not getting a splash down below, not getting a thing for all his efforts, what the hell good are those bluer-than-blues in the dark recesses of an outhouse hole when you're turning ninety-nine and everything's still trapped inside?

EVERY YEAR ON HIS BIRTHDAY from the time his birthday was designated the last great date of the aught years, True Bliss has served Kennesaw Belvedere his birthday tea, just the two of them, just the one day a year. In his early forties it became clear that his blue eyes were getting bluer by the year while all other eyes on him turned as pale as spit as the years advanced. Heads were put together, wits were gathered, and those whose minds had yet to turn to applesauce mush were asked to think as one to determine an appropriate display of awe for this unusual man and his growing-bluer-by-the-year eyes. True Bliss, by her own consensus and the force of a rolling pin, let it be known that as the oldest in town it would be she who would fete this man, this unusual man and his bluer-by-the-year eyes, this man three hundred and sixty-four days younger than herself. True alone would make the occasion of his birth, the tenth of the month, a date of infamy, and on this unique occasion she and she alone would be the one to serve Kennesaw Belvedere his birthday tea. Loma Soyle and Twosie Lope were a pair of scissors to True's unwritten decree about this last great date of the aught years, but True took a rock to their scissors and dismissed their complaints as merely pennies and pins, nothing but a drawer full of sheer nonsense, and with others too timid to offer any challenges of their own, True's insistence on tea for only two become law etched in legend.

True's own birthday, in the shadow of his day one day hence on the eleventh of the month, was never designated a great date of the aughts or any decade. She has been prepared to celebrate her century on the day following this one by her lone and only, with a hot apple slump and a whistle and cup of bicarbonate. But Kennesaw's birthday tea will come first.

THIRTY-SIX THOUSAND ONE HUNDRED and thirty-five days ago it was clear that Kennesaw Buckett Belvedere would stick out in town like a healthy thumb. As an infant newly disgorged into the world, he was a constant worry to his mother, Porcine, for neither his face nor body nor developing temperament reflected any familiar family traits, not one Belvedere-Minton-Bliss-Drell-Soyle-Hackensack-Whiskerhooven-Aspetuck-

Swampscott-Saflutis-Engersol-Lope-O'ums-Buckett
bit. With nary a recognizable protuberance or tic, not
a horse laugh, not a limp, and most disturbingly, with
only ten fingers and toes in perfect tact, Porcine feared
that her only offspring with his bluer-than-blues and
chiseled cleft and long strong limbs would be subject to
ridicule, knuckle-pointing, and worse. Others in town
were giving birth in the years that followed to children more un-comely, yet recognizable, and it pained
Porcine so to see her Kennesaw growing more poised
and proportional as the years slipped on. She'd see hoo-
ligans in town, the unfairly unremarkable younger boys
with their flipper noses and their heads like butternut
squashes, stop and gape at her Kennesaw as he passed
their way like a June breeze through March, and they'd
line up behind him and mimic his sure footsteps and
follow him wherever he went with what she was certain
was silent derision. Porcine's only glimmer of hope was
that the girls of town reacted much as she had in his
early days, overcome by the disturbing sight of him and
fainting until he and the torment of him passed.

Kennesaw never seemed to notice his effect on others, shrugged off any reactions as just folk being folk,
pointed his bluer-than-blues ahead of him and beyond
and walked tall and oblivious to the thump-thump under his feet that was his mother's heart. Porcine wept
herself into eternal sleep from heartache—that's what

people told themselves. Her last thought was that boys such as Kennesaw were as wasteful as a gold strike in a town that prized coal.

KENNESAW THINKS OF HIS MOTHER as he sits on the privy. He recalls the frequency with which he rebuffed her advances on him with ax blades and pitchforks. He pushes with all his might to rid his body of the memory of dinners of boiled rocks and of pots of scalding water spilled his way, *accidentally*. He thinks thoughts as dark as the slop beneath him of her tears and her sudden tantrums, and the conversations she often had in rooms that were empty of others. He pushes and he pushes through his memories, yet nothing comes of his efforts but a sharp interior pain. He squeezes his guts and pushes harder and a new stitch of pain makes him think of his father now, too. Of how Flummox Belvedere called him Blue Eyes. The sound of it still echoes in the darkest parts of Kennesaw's heart. The disapproval in the sound of *blue*. The dress down of it. *You, Blue Eyes,* his father would taunt as he unfastened his belt, that strip of an unjust god, *get over here*.

Kennesaw peers between his thighs into the dark reflection below him, seeing his father's loosening belt and his mother's flying iron, and shaking his head with disbelief that such thoughts still swirl in him freely while other things in him take a prune enema to dislodge. Overalls around his ankles, slunk low on the can with his eyes scrunched shut as he groans through a push, the slightest malodor escapes his cemented pucker and ascends to sting him in one of those bluer-than-blues. What he's put in to these ninety-nine years is stored up inside of him and push after gut-pained push he can't get it out, none of it, never could.

KENNESAW THINKS: THEY SAY ninety-nine is as good as a hundred, better even, sounds like a bigger number, the pair of nines, two bent backs and stooped over heads resting on sagging chests, what an old couple; take two walking sticks and jab 'em right through those nine eyes and make 'em see a hundred stars before dark. You can keep your ninety-nine, keep your hundred, take back the last twenty even and leave me be with eighty at best, the last twenty have been one long indignity of branches dying on the tree of me, and rot at the root now trickling out of the birthday boy. Won't this be a gift for True: if I'm lucky, I won't live another year and she'll get to be one hundred forever, all by herself.

Kennesaw hates thinking: ninety-nine. Can't even get this last week out of him and into the can. Worse still, there's an alarming little sting down there that closing his eyes tight in pain does not remedy. It could be from anything. It could be from the push. It could be a nettle he swallowed. It could be the memory of his father, lodged in his gut for eternity.

Kennesaw doesn't know what to think: ninety-nine. He came into this world with seventy-eight functioning organs and at least a dozen of them no longer work properly, yet he's here, he's still here. He may not have been born with any outward signs of family resemblance, but his innards call each other cousin. So what if he has the Hackensack-or-Is-It-Whiskerhooven gallbladder with its annual stone toss, or the Buckett heart that couldn't keep a steady beat if you stretched it on a drum. He's still here. True's still here. Hunko Minton is still here. Hunko was always still here. Carnival Aspetuck—is he still here? Or Frainey Swampscott? Either Soyle sister? Whoever is left, we're here. We're all that's left and we're all that's here. A spread of ninety to one day shy of one hundred, so many years, too many years, and in not too many more our numbers will be up.

And now this: a stopped-up old man on the can with his overalls down around his ankles and his will to live lower than that. It's his birthday. He's ninety-nine. Perhaps True's tea will slippery his slopes. If he pulls up his overalls and cinches his belt, his father's belt, that strip of an unjust god, and runs a brush through the pewter on his head and pinches his cleft and chisel for spirit and blinks his bluer-than-blues to put the sparkle back in them, he'll be ready for the trek to True's for his birthday tea; that loosening tea; he'd drink the paint flakes off her parlor ceiling if they'd get what's inside of him out for good.

He thinks sometimes what you put into a life you'll never get out. He flats a palm on the privy door and steps out into the morning light, blinks his bluer-than-blues, breathes in his ninety-nine, wipes his hands of what just happened. His birthday is the last great date of the aughts and he's due at True's to celebrate the occasions of his life. It'll take him some time to get there, and hopefully, not too long to get home.

3: HUNKO

HUNKO MINTON ROSE WITH THE DAY like it was the last of Creation. The day and what was to come came in fresh as a hen's egg with a slight breeze from the south and no more precipitation in the air than a hummingbird's pee. The sun did what the sun usually does on an Indian summer Thursday: took its sweet time to rise by 6:17, yawned and scratched itself until 7:05, and by 8:23 deigned to fling its arms wide and stick out its big yellow tongue and claim the day officially on. At one minute past nine if you were that blue sky and you wanted to hurry up and idle, you had no need for a shave or a bath, and no need to brush your pearly whites clean of stardust, your skin was corn silk and your breath sweet chrysanthemum.

Hunko excreted an altogether different aroma. Waking and stretching and scratching and poking out more than a yellow tongue, Hunko arose with a prehistoric agenda. He and the funk of him bypassed the kitchen pump and its cool runnings in favor of a quick head dunk into the last of last week's rainwater left murky in the barrel out back of his kitchen door. You'd think he'd be whapping the bejitters out of all the mosquitoes flocking above the green-hued pool, but leathered skin like his is a callused shell impervious to sticks and pricks, and if they bit him he'd let them, today was not about flies.

Hunko grabbed his hose; his bladder needed bleeding. He bowlegged it to the privy beside the well, but mistook the left-leaning pump house for the left-leaning outhouse, and disabused himself of enough flood to drown a turkey—disabused it right into the only semi-clean water on his land. He slid a wet finger across his mossy teeth then ran his tongue to follow, and the pee-yew of it was all the reminder he needed that today would be as different a bird as any that had ever flown.

A million years ago today it was the day for grounding pterodactyls, or so Hunko decided, and he woke this morning in full bore meteor to reenact the anniversary. On every tenth of September since the molten lava cooled, True Bliss served tea and saltines to Kennesaw Belvedere in the parlor of her home on the occasion of his birth, and this was the day, and that was the deed, and he, Hunko Minton, was going to be the blast that would finally end that repast.

Looking back, there had been, from Hunko's perspective, between himself and Kennesaw, a vision of the future in which the two of them viewed the horizon through a conjoined set of eyes—a future as only a cyclops could see it—without worry, without censure and, without question, without others. That this did not come to pass—yet—was something Hunko in his youth did not see coming, nor could he endure the ongoing sight of it in his young manhood, but unlike the fabled Cyclops whose powers were lost in a single blinding blow, Hunko has never lost his focus on the horizon and the dream he knows will one day rise there before his eyes, and that day is this one.

All through the long stretch of his young adult years through his middle years he endured Kennesaw's inexplicable daily disappearances from not only his life but also from town itself during daylight. As years grew mossy, and Kennesaw was once again inexplicably present in town, as if he'd never been absent for more than an afternoon, though not necessarily present in Hunko's daily life, what set Hunko atavistic was what he sensed to be the growing bill and coo between Kennesaw and True Bliss. At picnics, at cart-arounds, Kennesaw couldn't so much as pinch a crease in his overalls without True's eyes ironing him. One Sunday not so many years ago (in truth, it could have been more than fifty), he witnessed them passing one another in front of the windows at New Eden Grangery and caught True espying Kennesaw's sidelong glances at his own reflected self in the only piece of plate glass not broken, and seeing that, Hunko hurt like his own face had broken the rest, and the hurt he felt from that, like the broken glass, has never mended. True Bliss and her wandering cataracts had no business doing such wanton admiring, and although there was no proof that Kennesaw was the least bit aware of her awareness, Hunko decided he had to keep an eye on them both.

Morning and its sleepy smell waddled fat and lazy through ten o'clock, then eleven o'clock, and needing a rest after such inert exertion, straddled its ass on noon like a buzzard on a fence rail. By one o'clock the southern breeze was starting to heckle a bit, and by 1:40 it was a full-blown bossy gale. Hunko was undeterred by the air and its growing discontent. In full snit, he was a disruption of molecules as he stampeded through the overgrown clearing where four generations of Drells were felled; his anger falling all over itself on the ridge where all the girls used to tumble in the high grasses that aren't grasses anymore; and he was coming undone by the time he stomped along the shores of Grunts Pond where the males of every generation first took themselves in hand and learned what they were capable of, and where Hunko's youth-ignited Kennesaw obsession first issued from the depths of him. Today's outrage would quell it once and for all and put a life-lasting longing to bed. He was sure of it.

By the time he reached the lumpy west slope of the valley beyond Grunts Pond, Hunko had become a geological disturbance: naming rocks True and kicking them. By two o'clock as the air picked up speed Hunko's pace did, too, kicking more rocks he named True, even kicking one he named Kennesaw but that was accidental, and the next True rock he kicked he blamed for it. By 2:13 his toes swole numb from so much kicking, by 2:28 as he bushwhacked his way through the tangles that devoured the pass from the old Drell barn to the old Buckett barn, which was between the old old Drell barn and the old old Buckett barn, and by the time he rounded the woodshed that was all that was left of the newest of the oldest Aspetuck barns, his anger was no longer something he could molt off like feathers, he was as drenched with it as he was with perspiration and neither smelled pretty.

Blind fury doesn't see what it needs to see, while the wind can stare holes anywhere it wants. Hunko squashed sucker pumpkins on his trespass through

Carnival Aspetuck's long-ago garden, right in front of where Carnival would be sitting if Carnival was still among the standing; but standing or sitting it wouldn't have mattered anyway. If Carnival had been standing there in the mist, he might have wobbled his old ax handle at Hunko in protest; towards his end, that was the best Carnival's once legendary grip would allow. He'd press a given-up fist to his gone-bad hip and lead with his good as he'd duck under the clothesline where his sister Jubilee's ample up-busters once hung to dry and he'd try to shoo Hunko from his gourds, but standing, sitting, shaking, even living—none of it would do no good. Hunko was all anger and stomp, well out of the garden and off on a diminishing trail of butternut by the time Carnival might have reached the carnage, had Carnival still been earthbound and erect. Best his ghost could hope for was a gust of wind to catch his sister's padded encasement and jumble it airborne like a swollen cloud till it found a landing spot abreast his own ectoplasmic face and brought him back to their life.

4. JUBILEE

ODD HOW GOING THROUGH LIFE as one of two should leave Jubilee Aspetuck feeling so alone, all the more so at the end.

Jubilee was a product of a harvest moon and two cousins in the shadows gone goofy. It was the kind of clandestine whoop-de-do that related townsfolk were adept at, and Jubilee's parents were definitely related and most decidedly adept. No one saw the union coming. Russet Aspetuck with his alluring cowlick and long thumbs had long been intended for Agapanthus Saflutis, and barring an intercession by Butte O'ums or Columbine Buckett, an Aspetuck-Saflutis union in the spring of whenever promised to be by all accounts a union free of the usual genetic flimflammery.

Russet Aspetuck, instructed by his father to bank in his heart a fire that would last a lifetime, chopped one hundred cords of maple and hickory and ash and oak, he stacked them high and spread them wide, and when he was done he confessed to his mother that he would rather see them burn to cinders than have to live long enough to heat the house of a bride he didn't want to wed. This was news no town crier had ear of, and the suddenness of it led his usually composed mother to take an ice pick to the locked spice box for a nip of vanilla bean and a swig of applejack.

Russet's father was of the mind that a groom is only nervous of that which he better not have had much if any practice at, and assured Russet that after a few years of pleading and sobbing and insisting and threatening he would figure out the ins and outs of husbandry and develop into a fine sire, if not a companionable mate, or at the very least something warm to thrust one's feet against.

Russet's heart sank as deep as the potato he was named for. There was nothing terrifically repulsive about Agapanthus Saflutis that could not be stomached after a tankard or two; she had a ready, if reedy, laugh, one or two of her fingertips were virgin skin never pierced while needle working, and the headache she was born with had grown in her an appreciation for solitude, darkness, and the calming effects of cats.

Had there been a rival for Russet's affections it was thought to be Columbine Buckett, whose bloom was considered more delicate and spirited, though she was easily swayed by any blowing wind. Columbine herself was promised to tried and true Butte O'ums, as regular a man as any who had ever wound a ball of string. Columbine Buckett was fond of Russet in the way one might favor a sweet potato over a yam, liked his cowlick and his long thumbs, yet her heart was not exactly set on fire by a second cousin who could chop one hundred cords of wood anymore than it was by a first cousin who knew his way around twine. Agapanthus Saflutis spent long hours under heavy cover—trees, horse blankets, the what mattered not—soothing her throbbing cranium and fully dreading a bent knee and a bouquet and a marry-me-do, and made no efforts to give Russet a reason to want her. Likewise Columbine Buckett, not in anymore of a marrying mood than Agapanthus or Russet or rock-solid Butte, but whose cold feet could use a warm back, reckoned if Butte could bend a knee, she could wiggle a toe. Why Columbine was seen as an asp at the bosom of Agapanthus's matrimonial bliss is anybody's guess, but loose tongues don't need the taste of reason to hiss.

All through the winter and into the spring of whenever, Russet restacked and restacked his one hundred cords of wood, turned the forest he had felled into an acre piled high, and thought the blisters on his palms and the splinters in his long thumbs would teach his heart not to be such a baby. As he stacked and restacked his cords of maple and hickory and ash and oak, enough to sustain a marriage or burn down the gates of hell, he practiced his kneeling and rehearsed his betrothing. Day after wood-stacking day, he'd fashion an effigy of Agapanthus out of a thick oak bole whose bark reminded him of her complexion, atop of which he sat a plop of earth and splintered grasses to approximate her hair. Before her he'd fall on one knee and then the other, shifting his weight from his right side to his left, which, after a long day of chopping and stooping and stacking, was no pain-free matter. Once in a picture book he'd seen a knight in dented armor kneeling in such a fashion before a blushing maiden fair, one hand beseeching her heart to join his while his other arm was folded behind his back with a bouquet ready to go, so Russet knelt and offered out to the unquartered log that was Agapanthus a callused hand with splintered thumb, and behind his back he hid the next best thing to a bunch of flowers that would soon be wilted anyway: his ax. Russet could have drawn on the words of better men, words kissed by cherubs and starlight, extolling the beauties of matrimony immortalis, as he rehearsed fully half of his heart in the time-honored entreaty that would make Agapanthus his own, but from the pit of his stomach came his own poetry sure to seal the deal. To her he entreated: "*Um, wanna?*"

Russet was no spud. He had his alluring cowlick and his long thumbs. He could chop wood, he had turned the pages of picture books, and he was scholarly to the fact that poetry is a fancy way of tying a noose. Surely among the family forest of trees there was a cousin more comely than Agapanthus whose feet he'd be happy to feel, someone whose bark wasn't dry and peeling, someone whose head wasn't always aching, someone who hated cats as much as he did. Russet informed his father and his mother and Agapanthus and her parents, too, that he'd wed once he was sure he had chopped enough wood to keep Agapanthus from growing cold to his touch.

Columbine Buckett wed Butte O'ums in early summer of whenever, and by autumn of that same ever, she and the old ball of twine were as surprised as any neighbor that inside her womb a small knot was growing. Russet hewed and felled and chopped and stacked and sweated and callused and counted, and once he was done and both families were satisfied that he'd chopped more trees than Lebanon had cedars, he hemmed and hawed and started again to hew and fell some more. His cowlick flattened from his outpouring of sweat and his long thumbs turned hard as spring branches. Agapanthus did not seem to mind the delay, only the noise from all that felling and yelling of *timber!*

By winter of the next whenever the Saflutis family could see the forest for all the felled trees. Russet Aspetuck was more interested in having his hands on his ax than on their daughter, and there was little reasoning with a man who was always off by himself swinging his ax. So Etingem Saflutis did what any father would do to avoid any chance that Agapanthus would make solitude and darkness her lifelong ambition and live out her years in his house like a truffle. He took down from the wall the blunderbuss handed down from his father from the set-to of '76, he oiled it and packed it tight with biscuits baked by Agapanthus herself (they were as hard as any scrap iron he might have used for ammunition), and set off for the woods to convince Russet to lay down his ax and give marriage the thumbs up. Etingem only intended to scare the lad into stopping his chopping, to lay down his ax long enough to bend down on one knee and take his daughter off his hands for good. But when he aimed the flared barrel at Russet, Russet raised his ax in defense, and somewhere in the altercation between blade and barrel and boom, the thumb he hoped would be up was shot off.

FOUR THUMBS A MARRIAGE MAKE, not three, and if Russet couldn't supply two, Agapanthus would hand over none. She had found in his dismemberment a reason not to wed, and to her parents' dismay and Russet's delight, an Aspetuck-Saflutis union would develop in the spring of when-never. As the last Saflutis, Agapanthus lived out her days needlepointing in solitary bliss and very little light, her headache miraculously cured, her womb as untilled as the fields her father bequeathed her. It was in her early middle years that she succumbed to a cat scratch gone gangrenous.

Russet, now, with one thumb less and too much wood, didn't know what to do with his ax. He still had his alluring cowlick and one long thumb, and that one long thumb was longer by far than any other thumb in town. Sometimes it's what we lack that makes us appealing, and Russet soon learned that there were cousins in town who liked him more now that he had one thumb less, and one cousin above all who couldn't wait to grab hold of it.

Circe Trousard was the siren of four families with a high bust and a come-hither shimmy. The Aspetucks and the Trousards had a common link through a Minton-Lope coupling that both sides could trace to the set-to of '76, when, under the red glare of bombs bursting in air, there was more being raised in the night than a flag. Circe Trousard had toyed with but tendered scant serious attention to other cousins paraded before her. She had been courted, cuddled by, and considered engaged at one time or another to Rufus Drell, who had more teeth than sense, and Hinkley Minton, with his sniffer like a third ear, and Intermediate Hurlbutt, who had fleas. For each one of these cousins in whom she found too much to not want, Circe took stock of their excessive faults and when they pressed for her hand she impressed back with her knee.

Circe Trousard never lacked for snaps and whistles, but as a girl who knew the worth and future a high bust buys, she preferred to hear her own raspy voice do the yoo-hooing. The spring of her eighteenth was the same spring Russet Aspetuck's thumb was blunderbusted, and no sooner was he bandaged and poulticed and unbetrothed, that Circe set her sights first on what he was lacking and then on what he had left. One long thumb was all a girl like Circe needed to make her insides sing like a wood thrush. Russet took one look at his overlooked cousin, saw her eyes bug and her bust heave, and experienced a stirring in his core like he never felt with his ax. It may have only been spring, but for the both of them: what a fall!

Nine months to the full moon when they first warmed their feet on one another, Circe gripped Russet's long thumb with all her might and screamed and kicked and sweated and peed and heaved into the world the celebration of their cousinhood: their first born: their Jubilee. Not a week passed before Circe's toes caught a chill and she gave Russet the thumbs up to warming her feet anew, and the heat he was only too happy to resume generating was hotter than any two hundred cords could ignite. Their daughter Jubilee was two months shy of her first birthday when her brother Carnival came into her world and wouldn't leave her alone.

JUBILEE ASPETUCK NEVER HAD much of a season as the only apple of her parents' eyes. With her brother Carnival hot on her heels, this new worm out of their mother's womb left her feeling like a shadow and not the sun.

Carnival had a cry louder than a screech owl and was talking before Jubilee had even buckteethed. He inherited his father's alluring cowlick and his long thumbs, too, and got from his mother the Lope appetite and the Minton indifference to table manners. He grew sooner than Jubilee and bigger in under a year, and fast as Circe could stitch his swaddling, Carnival was out of nightshirts and out of knickers and out of his seat at the dinner table, hogging every last turnip, hen toe, and gizzard. He was a big boy from the word go, and like his father, crack with an ax. By five, he was chopping saplings like plucking daisies; by ten he could split an oak and have it stacked before noon. Kids will be kids, but a kid with an ax is about as adult as they come. Carnival swung it from sunup to set every day but the Sabbath, and every family in town needed a man to chop and he was the boy for the job. When he wasn't swinging his ax he was reaching for the whole fresh loaf of life and dragging it unsliced through a pan of drippings, then sucking his long thumbs of every last drop, lickety-split. He chopped and ate and chopped and ate; he outgrew his long johns with shoulders too broad for doorways and split his britches with thighs two sizes too thick. Carnival wasn't all that tall, but he filled space like a heat wave, leaving little room for his big sister.

By contrast, Jubilee was small—a stunted bud to a full-blown bloom. To make the most of her compact size, she was heir to her mother's high bust and her father's long thumbs and cowlick, and as luck would have it, she was blessed with both buckteeth and knock-knees, but on the whole: not bad. Where her brother had size and sharp steel to make his points, Jubilee could speak plenty with just a look. She had eyes as expressive as a sky turning storm; she'd never have to say much.

Russet and Circe were parents like any other parents. They fed their children, they clothed their children, they taught their boy how to be a man and their daughter how to be useful. Before they warmed their feet at night they knelt by their bed and prayed for a son-in-law who would not be too related. About Carnival they had no qualms. Carnival had his ax and his future stacked up before him, and as long as there was wood and food and someone to tend his darker wants, he'd want for nothing in this world.

When it was courting time, they advised Carnival as Russet's father had advised him: to bank in his heart a fire that would last a lifetime, to chop and stack an acre square and to find himself a foot-warmer with whom to spend eternity sparking. Carnival took broad canvas of his options: there was True Bliss and Frainey Swampscott and Zebelia Was-She-a-Hackensack-or-Was-She-a-Whiskerhooven, though he sensed not a one of them appreciated a man with an ax. There was bent-necked Petie Soyle and her equally twisted sister, Loma, though neither saw much in him, Petie least of all. There were all three Lopes, each unlovelier than the last, despite their enticingly big feet. And empty-headed as a thimble there was Butte and Columbine's little O'ums, Knotsy, who was as pale and permeable as a jellyfish and about whom the less said was always so much the better. As cousins go, any one of these lasses would make a fine bride. Never mind the certainty that the further narrowing of the bloodlines might produce something more mineral than animal, Russet and Circe secretly hoped that the pride of their loins would till Loma Soyle, even if what grew was a vegetable, and a vegetable would be a far sight better than another see-through Knotsy O'ums.

But Carnival had his ax set elsewhere. No one curled his toes more than his own sister.

5: Hunko

Before Grunts Pond was Grunts Pond it was Lake Minton and before it was Lake Minton it must have had a native name like Big Small or Waters of Loud Echoes or Pocahontas's Pool or some other name no white man would have had history enough to come up with. Depending on who tells the tale, Mintons were here almost from the time Blisses and Belvederes were here, or Blisses were here almost from the time Belvederes and Mintons were here, doesn't really change how the body of water got its name, all three families agree it was in the winter when they all arrived, everything was covered with snow, there was ice but not thick ice, and it was Hezekiah Minton who went out in his snowshoes in search of something to eat so his wife and infant son wouldn't starve, and because he didn't know the lay of the land like the natives did, he trundled right out into the flat middle of a wide open snowy space where no trees grew and before you could say gitchigoomie, the flat wide open space opened up just enough to swallow Hezekiah whole. The echo from his final words bounced around the snow bowl and effervesced through the trees and it was a Bliss or a Belvedere if it was anyone who heard his yelp before he went glub glub to the bottom.

It was late spring at the earliest when the snow melted enough to reveal the little ice that remained and the waters underneath the ice, and it was late summer at the earliest when the water's level dropped to a dipper and there in the cracked mud of the dried-up bed were the bones of Hezekiah Minton and on his feet the snowshoes that didn't help him one damn bit. The infant son he left behind was named Horatio and he begat a son named Hudson who begat a son named Harmon who begat a son named Hyman who begat a son named Hinkley who begat the son named Herkimer whom we know as Hunko.

Because Hezekiah's rib cage was only half out of the dried mud and half stuck in it, it was agreed upon by those who found him that his remains should remain where they remained; and because no marker could

reasonably be erected, the body of water that had re-
ceded to a dipper but which would come back by the
time the autumn rains returned, they decided, would be
marker enough, and so they called it Lake Minton. Their
decision to call it Lake Minton and not Lake Hezekiah
was based in part on the assumption that anyone stupid
enough to trudge out into the flat middle of a wide open
snowy space where no trees grew and not figure there
was probably water underneath would probably beget
offspring equally as ignorant and why limit a name to
one fool when you can honor his entire family?

Lake Minton stayed Lake Minton through Horatio's
time and Hudson's time and Harmon's time, but it was
around the time of Hyman's time when the waters started earning an unofficial nickname not actually named
by Hyman but inspired by Hyman and other boys in
town like Hyman, all of whom would go down to the
rocky shores of the big small lake and from random
points work up lonely utterances that echoed across the
waters and oozed through the trees and were instant-
ly recognized by all who heard them as rutting grunts.
Because these grunts ceased to cease and only grew
louder and more frequent when Hyman's son Hinkley
and other boys like him took up the habit with ferocious
regularity, Lake Minton thus became known unofficially
as Lake Grunt, and because they were captivated by the
notion of renaming it a name less formal it was decided

too that the lake really was no lake in size, it was more of a pond, and should be referred to as such, and in short order, it became not just a pond it became Grunts Pond, and although no maps were changed, it's been called that ever since.

Hinkley Minton and the other boys like him—Flummox Belvedere and Righteous Whiskerhooven and Rufus Drell and Bull Engersol and Russet Aspetuck and Boyle Lope and Pernicious Upland and Intermediate Hurlbutt and Etingem Saflutis and Butte O'ums and Remedial Bliss—they all passed through that awkward stage from seedlings to saplings at their random points by the rocky shores of Grunts Pond with their rutting grunts growing louder and more frequent the closer to manhood they came. A boy in town who didn't learn what he was capable of doing all by his lonesome when he was off by his lonesome on the rocky shores of Grunts Pond doing it was about as rare in these parts as a man named Bob. The only difference between Hinkley Minton and the other boys like him who learned what they were capable of when they were off by their lonesome learning it and the boys whom they begat is, was, and forever will be that Hinkley and his friends got to put their learning to use, which was how the boys they begat were begotten. The boys whom they begat, Mawz Engersol and Carnival Aspetuck and Kennesaw Belvedere and Luddy Upland and Elementary Hurlbutt

49

and Brisket Whiskerhooven and Hunko Minton, all went to that same school by the rocky shores of Grunts Pond and learned what they were capable of when off by their lonesomes (the girls all flocked to Tumblers' Ridge to tickle their ever-mores); only, no one they knew of short of whom they have their suspicions about, has ever put their learning to use beyond perfecting the art of being off by their lonesomes—and if there's one artist among all who was ever off by his lonesome most often becoming the lonesome-est artist of all, that lonesome-est artist of all is Hunko Minton.

There have been few days in his last many thousands when Hunko has forgone his solitary excursion to the rocky shore of Grunts Pond to prove to himself yet anew what he already knows he's capable of all by his lonesome. From late spring to early autumn this daily bit of business enjoys a warm hand in the warm air warming the slick, and the grunts he finishes up with show as much gratitude to the favorable climate as they do to the final outcome. One would think, however, that the extended cold snap from late autumn to early spring might induce such an outdoor enthusiast to either forgo his daily habit or take it inside, but Hunko has never been guided by a head full of sense. As the autumn trees blow their loads of leaves all over the place and the naked branches chuckle in the wind, Hunko can be heard not just grunting by his lonesome but chattering by his lonesome from icy hands and chilly friction, and once the real cold sets when the first snow covers the land in a thick creamy coat of white, the sounds that linger in the frosty air like an extra-cold blast are Hunko by his lonesome chattering his way to his solitary, if shrunken, accomplishment, finished off with a short, shivered grunt.

For a smudge of a man like Hunko Minton to stand with his drawers down around his boots in snow up to his knees, shivering by his lonesome just for the sake of proving to himself what he can do by his lonesome out-doors on a daily basis, weather come-what-may, takes balsam—the smell of balsam. Trees. The assault on his senses, that blast of earthen fresh is what first makes his nerve endings tingle, and by the time his whole sys-tem is infused with the aroma, his resolve stiffens to the daily task at hand, and he is compelled to beat his way through whatever elements arise until on the rocky shores of Grunts Pond he accomplishes what he came for. Balsam is the scent of his earliest recall, it was the scent placed in his infant crate to diffuse the scent of him. It's the scent that envelops most of the town in a year-round vapor of campfires and sleigh bells, and the scent and the sensation it elicits in him are what Hunko most associates with Kennesaw Belvedere.

Kennesaw was already well accomplished at his own lonesome capabilities down by the rocky shores of

Grunts Pond when Hunko was still in short pants loaded with balsam. There was balsam in the air wherever Kennesaw strode and strutted, and on the tail wind of it, Hunko rode like a ribbon. Not so many years exist between them that would make friendship an improbability at that time of their lives, and although they weren't thick as thieves, they stole a few moments together here and there. A boy barely out of nappies can be just as much company to a stripling learning about his own sap as a chicken can be companion to a wolf, and Hunko would cluck after Kennesaw wherever Kennesaw went until Kennesaw's feathers got ruffled, whereupon Hunko, if he didn't act fast enough, he'd learn what it was like to get plucked. Kennesaw made it clear to Hunko that the rocky shores of Grunts Pond were no place for a boy in short pants, and until he was of an age where long pants down around his ankles were still longer than short pants pulled up, he was not to step foot anywhere nearby. It was assumed that Hunko heeded these warnings, for he was not to be seen by Kennesaw when Kennesaw was engaged in what he was capable of when off by his lonesome, yet if Kennesaw wasn't so engaged in what he was capable of he might have noticed the lad crouched behind a rock all those years on the rocky shore watching his every move and sniffing the air of its balsam while attempting to learn for himself if he himself was capable of anything yet.

It was a considerable stretch of time before Hunko was capable of anything when off by his lonesome, and the day he first discovered what he was capable of, the day he was first capable of it, was also the first day Kennesaw was aware that Hunko was following his every daily move. Hunko had been careful to keep his presence unknown and his sounds unheard, his every sniff of balsam was the slightest whiffle of a breeze, his every little hand friction the ripple of a leaf. The sounds for which the pond was named were sounds he had certainly grown familiar with—they could be heard in a chain of polyphonic eruptions around the full circle of rocky shoreline at all hours of day and night, and after many, many, many outings crouched behind his rock, Hunko grew familiar with each distinct utterance and could tell you which boy in town uttered which particular grunt. Skilled as he became at listening, Hunko didn't care about the euphoniousness of the other individuals' grunts per se, his only real affection was for the resonant grunts of one person alone, and that person was Kennesaw, and since the first time he hid behind the rock and peeked, Hunko had looked forward to the day when he could imitate the sounds that came out of Kennesaw when Kennesaw's capabilities reached their peak. To Hunko's great surprise, the sound that ultimately debuted out of him on the day he was first capable of anything was a sound unlike any he had heard from anywhere around the shoreline; and to his even greater chagrin, as dissimilar to the sounds out of Kennesaw as morning dewdrops are to a flood. Granted, all grunts come from the same place. How they shoot out of one's soul when one is off realizing one's capabilities, the distinct individuality of their tone and propulsion from person to person is something the ancient Greeks must have studied and maybe even etched on a pot. What issued from Hunko's depths was not so much a grunt as it was a cough, a scratchy hack that was more befitting of clearing one's throat than of realizing one's full potential.

Who was more startled? Hunko: because of what came out of him, vocally and otherwise? Or Kennesaw: because he wasn't alone and hadn't yet finished? The way Luddy heard it, Hunko barely had time to fasten his snaps before Kennesaw hoisted the little interloper by his balsam and lobbed him into the pond. Jubilee told Petie Soyle that Carnival said that Kennesaw later told him that he was so fully engaged in his lonesome and so taken by surprise that not only had he reached his full potential much sooner than he would have wanted to but that he reached it with a velocity and span that would have required depiction by the ancient Greeks not on a pot but on a very long frieze. Jubilee told Onesie Lope that Carnival then told her that he wasn't just talking about a span from his nose to his toes, but a length of yards from where he stood to where Hunko hid and it hit the kid in the eye, and that *that* was the real surprise to them both.

YOU COULD HAVE A STICK in your hand or a fishing rod, or an ax or a fire-poker or a pistol, and it won't ever mean you've come to grips with yourself the way having yourself in hand makes you who you are. On that day Hunko discovered about himself a longing that was inbred and immutable and it fixated on Kennesaw and it wouldn't let go. It had been in him in his infancy, it was the tickle in his ribs and the gist of his ism, and it rimmed him in crimson for the rest of his life.

A curiosity is something you sample and set free. Kennesaw saw this as a passing interest that Hunko would get his fill of and forget, and so he indulged his young friend in shoreside sessions of mutual lonesomeness—not every day, but getting close. He felt heroic, Kennesaw; Hunko seemed so taken by his mien and measure that it swelled his intentions and thrilled the performer in him in a way no isolated outing ever did. Kennesaw rose to the occasion out of his own curiosity about curiosity, and in Hunko's adulation of him, he found that his capability for reaching his full potential was double what it had ever been before. Kennesaw could go either way about curiosity. If he didn't like a

bean, he tasted it and spat it out. If a beaver waddled his
way he might give it a damn, he might not. But this curiosity was an entirely different animal, and he couldn't
deny that he was in its cage.

Hunko never has had the ability to see one thing as
two things, to see bars as a fence, to see a cage as a trap.
What is is what is, and it is without question, and if there
are objections to his understanding of it or his embrac-
ing of it, he is dumb to them. If Kennesaw had let him,
Hunko would have devoted all hours of every day to
the care and feeding of his feelings for his idol, he would
have run through town leaving a streak of opalescence
declaring the day begun with Kennesaw's first breath
and completed with his eyelid's last bat. If Kennesaw
had let him, which he did not, Hunko would have
looped a cordon of his own intestines around his heart-
sake to keep others from nearing, and he would have
done this to show the depths of his heart while dumb to
the extremes of the act. Days down by the rocky shore
Kennesaw indulged and Hunko adored and together
their capabilities reached new heights and high as they
went Hunko dreamed they'd go higher still. Kennesaw
fully expected the fancy to pass, not only from Hunko
but from himself, and when it didn't he was as startled
as the day he discovered Hunko hunkered and hacking,
and his surprise turned to fear when thoughts of his father's disapproval clouded his bluer-than-blue-eyed

wonder, and as Flummox reared upon Kennesaw, Kennesaw's fear turned mean upon Hunko, and instead of laying his arm around the lad he stiffened the length of it between them.

Days down by the rocky shore would continue—not every day, not even close, not anymore—and although Kennesaw kept his hand in for a while longer, clearly his heart was someplace else. Hunko didn't understand how this one thing could be another thing—if he had done something rash, said something wrong, been more vocal, used less friction, shown more capability, surely the lesson would be learned, Kennesaw would teach him bad from better and there would be a lifetime of days like the days that came before. But all that came after were fewer days and shorter ones, and on more of those Kennesaw would participate less and less, and one day he stopped coming all together, and Hunko was left to reach his own potential all by his lonesome. It's been that way ever since. Every day, down on the rocky shore of Grunts Pond. The smell of balsam and Hunko in its thrall, and his heart still bursting with Kennesaw. You'd think an obsession like this would have climaxed long ago.

6: Kennesaw

Flummox Belvedere stepped anywhere he damn well pleased and land knew to bow and water to wave. His arms pumped high and his boots grounded firm and he was locomotive on his way to wherever, and should you come upon him in town or field or wood it was your business to lie down or get out of his way. As stepped the father, such steps were the steps of Kennesaw's youth and manhood; up until only a decade or so ago his own steps were direct and proud and manifest in their destiny to make the earth tread lightly around him. The change in those steps in his past ten years give shape to his steps this morning of his ninety-ninth, tentative steps, each one needing a breath all its own. It gives him pause that his long limbs can no longer stride the length of town in less time than it takes the day to blink its first—serious pause, since he needs to rest more often than every so.

The mere thought of the walk ahead to True's and his body so out of oil is enough to make him wish the calendar year had one less day: this. Before there's the town to no longer stride well across, there's the woods; and before the woods, the clearing where the Drells were felled; and before the clearing more woods; and before those Saflutises' fields; and in the shadow of the near-by Tumblers' Ridge is Grunts Pond, where the boy in him discovered his own manhood and more, then more woods; and one last wood; and on the edge of those the old back road; and before that the unpaved ruts that snake their way to his front fence with its broken gate and the tangle of overgrowth between the fence and the house; before all that there's the hip-aching business of just stepping out of his front door down and onto the granite mass below it, a mossy slab cold chiseled by hand by his great-grandfather, Congress, and set in place long before there was a house or door to step into. Six inches below the threshold when laid and now more than a foot drop to make that step down, the way things have settled. He'll grab the doorframe by its jamb and slowly lower one leg to the stone like stepping onto a boat on bobbing waters, then step his other leg down and let go of the doorframe and stand a moment to make sure the craft doesn't sink. Such a long journey ahead to walk to True's house for his birthday tea and just the thought of stepping out his front door is exhausting, and he hasn't even turned the knob.

One arm pumps and then the other. One leg shuffles and then the other. One ache and then another and then another and then another and this is how the aged walk into heaven.

Ache by ache Kennesaw makes his way through the late season milkweeds that make their own forest of his front yard, a chaos his own father would have seen to scything, down the trough of his front path to the broken gate of his front fence that in his dotage is a constant rebuke for his indifference. The sun takes pity on his slow progress and dims behind a surly cloud; it's a mercy to anyone but a blind man. In its absence, Kennesaw makes out a fuzzy shape beneath the overgrowth and attempts to wrestle upright and free of its binding thistles the sagging half-gate and losing the match mutters the same *be damned* that he has every other time he's wrestled it and lost in the last he-doesn't-know-how-many years. Might as well ask him where the other half-gate went, his brain won't budge on an answer to that either. Time and again he stubs his toe in the very same spot at the missing gate's opening and time and again it's the missing half suffocated under another thatch of weeds he stubs it on, but don't tell him to step aside, step around, there's another way through, there's another way out, this is the way to freedom and he can't recall any other, *be damned!*

What he does recall is that together the two gate halves made two halves of a heavenly harp, carved by hand and curved through sweat with slats like strings. Hunko Minton fashioned them with hand tools and found wood from a fallen tree back when making things out of found wood calmed his heart, toted them over, hung them and swung them as a surprise for Kennesaw, and as a surprise for them both, made a matching pair that he hung from the gate to his own home. He did this not long after Flummox Belvedere became nothing but a bad memory in a wooden box in a hole in Nedewen Field.

At the time, Kennesaw was impressed with the artistry and initiative and even said so out loud. Hunko might amount to something after all, he noted to Luddy Upland and Luddy told this to Carnival and Carnival told the rest. Such high praise when it made its way back to Hunko made Hunko puppy happy for more time than the compliment meant. Didn't last more than sixty years, though, the gates, since they were installed—Hunko must not have cared for Kennesaw all that much, Kennesaw said, or been too fine a carpenter, he added, if shoddy workmanship shows so soon. Good thing, he concluded early on, that Hunko stuck his talents where they wouldn't show for long: in the business of making boxes for the departed, which was how he put it to Threesie Lope, who couldn't bite her tongue quick enough when she told it to True in True's front parlor with the oriel window open and Hunko outside and below it, pressed against the south wall all fallen ears. The broken gate doesn't budge anymore than the splinter of regret Kennesaw has that he ever spoke such harsh words.

The sun slips out from its hiding and lights a fire under Kennesaw that he'd better make time. As the earth rotates one way, his four limbs sputter the other at the exact same speed, away from the gate and the freedom that brings to mind, and out onto the road, and into a different rut he knows well. With so little between his skin and bones, where there'd be room to store water is anybody's guess, yet perspiration slicks his brow and mucks under his arms and he can even feel his wattle below getting yeasty. Out of his house and away from his yard and only just beginning, to be this winded already you'd think it was miles and not minutes.

DOWN THE ROAD and down some more and more again; to compare his pace to a snail's would be slanderous to the snail. But in that shell he might as well be carrying on his back is Flummox Belvedere and his belt, that strip of an unjust god, and the sweaty game of Adam and Abel that he forced Kennesaw to play that Kennesaw couldn't leave home and run from fast enough. He recalls the first time Flummox was waiting for him in the doorway to the barn, looking both ways to see that no other soul was in presence. Kennesaw couldn't have been more than a squirt then, still in short pants—that much he's sure of. *Know what happens when I take off this belt?* his father would ask him, as he led the boy to a crib behind a stall in the back of the darkening barn; unbuckling, unslinging, unsmiling. The first time it happened Kennesaw didn't know the meaning, but with frequency he came to. It was not disapproval of his blue-eyed son, Kennesaw discovered, that burned through his father's body. It was something far more unsettling. Down the road and down some more and more again, as far from his father's clutches as a smart trout from a barbed hook. The refuge Kennesaw sought at True's as a boy gives his legs the lift they need to reach her house today.

ON HIS HEELS AS HE VEERS off the back road under the high sun is the man Kennesaw swore he'd always outrun. On the footpath worn to a scrape through the fields once farmed by families he cannot readily bring back to mind, those arms swing high and the boots grind firm and get closer. In the woods he passes the stumps of trees that once were thick enough to hide behind, yet now without their protection he can feel a hot breath on his neck and it distills him like the smell of whiskey on his father's. The canopy above is cheesecloth for filtering out the sun's stronger rays, but Kennesaw's shirt is collared in sweat and his breathing is deep and raspy and his chest is on fire and his sphincter not only stings but itches now and it sends shivers up him. The sun has never been able to warm this kind of chill out of him.

7: MAWZ

IF MEMORY SERVES, the last time True Bliss ever ate her own words was the summer Threesie Lope picked every last jack-in-the-pulpit from here to the end of forever and left them on True's front porch with a soot-signed note reading "ME." True was not accustomed to getting either flowers or notes, disdained the folly of both in fact, and viewed the freshly wilting blooms with their bulbous onion roots as not only unsought but unsightly. The note, which said nothing more than "ME" in handwriting that would put a chicken to shame, was no more welcome than the hooded pinks in their greenery, and if she knew who "ME" was, she'd sure give him or her the evil eye.

It was too early in the morning to be finding your front stoop festooned with an abundance of nature not to your liking, and whoever was the culprit or culprits to lay all these pulpits on her porch must have done so in the cool before sunrise because the petals were only just starting to curl when she opened her front vestibule door at dawn and found them. Someone creeping to her house in the wee hours—this was not good. Had she known that it was Threesie Lope, the only Lope triplet she liked, but the Lope triplet she trusted least, True would have marched across two fields to confront her friend, given her a piece of her mind and a slap. But True had no way of knowing that the jackanapes was Threesie, so the words stayed on her tongue and the sting remained on her palm.

True Bliss was not a woman who liked to waste a good tongue-lashing. It galled her all day that she didn't know whom to blame for the pile on her porch. It galled her when she mashed the screen door into the mound, it galled her as she kicked every last leaf down her steps, the slime on her boot galled her, the sludge on her steps galled her, the mush pile of it all galled her to such distraction that she didn't even have the wherewithal to clear away the mess. It sat in the sun at the foot of her steps and baked the day away until it turned into a smear of slimy sludge, and the evening breeze lifted the funk of it and wafted it through her front parlor oriel and shoved it up her nose. Some people conjure up the past by biting on a cookie, but True required more substantial means to put her mind back where she had come from, and there's nothing more substantial than a stinky odor on a hot summer night to send yourself running for cover.

Once long ago True had expected Mawz Engersol to tap-tap-tap on the opaque glass of her front vestibule door and escort her to the New Eden Grangery for the annual summer dance. It was the last summer of summer dances, it was the last dance of all dances, though no one could have known that then, and it was the last summer that True was in the high flush of her life, at the tail end of young, and not quite into the next uncertain age. She was upstairs in her bedroom in front of the small oval looking glass on her washstand admiring in its reflection the crest of her youth, prettying herself with a pink velvet ribbon, which she carefully threaded through her braid. It was a warm night, not steaming, and she left the high collar of her blouse unbuttoned to catch what cool there was; she'd finish the fasteners when she heard Mawz tap. In those days, True hummed. Little tunes that eddied in her imagination and ruminated in the air of her throat. Mawz was due at eight, but the clock at the foot of the stairs in the front entry hall had chimed eight nine or ten minutes back, and True became aware that her feelings had a look she wasn't too pleased with, that even this slight annoyance caused the skin around her eyes and mouth to pinch like milk skim. She tried, and succeeded, to hum the annoyance off her face and smoothed back her features to where they had lain serene; she felt a ripple of air on the pink of her neck and it was rejuvenating, and if Mawz Engersol were to arrive at this very moment he would see her now at the happiest she had ever looked in her life.

The air downstairs had a stifle to it, and her mother was the cause. Cozy was in a snit that her daughter was in a pet, mooning over a suitor and a summer dance. Whether it mattered that he was a cousin or a suitor plain and simple was debatable to True; her mother's foul mood didn't need a rational reason to fuel it anymore than a witch needs a broom to make soup. Cozy was a Bliss and her departed husband was a Bliss and her daughter was a Bliss two times over for more reasons than she could count and Mawz Engersol had Bliss in his bones and all this Bliss was probably too much Bliss to go around for her mother's liking. And then of course, there was the other thing.

Cozy had instructed her daughter from an early age

not to trust men, not to like them, and for pity's sake not to wallow in the moonlight with them; the male of the species is a ruination to every female—if Eve hadn't been so selfless and not shared her apple with that man, that business in Eden might never have turned the world topsy. Cozy had warned her daughter from an early age to mind her apples around just about every boy in town she knew, because every boy in town she knew was related to her in more ways than she realized and it was time the related stopped relating. *Keep away from Kennesaw Belvedere and Luddy Upland and Hunko Minton, not that that would be a sacrifice, from Carnival Aspetuck (if he could keep himself away from Jubilee), and more than anyone, don't go near Mawz Engersol, I'm warning you,* Cozy said more than once.

For many years, True did as she was warned, kept her distance kept her composure kept herself out of moonlight shadows and other equally iniquitous environs, if she saw a boy she crossed to the opposite side of the street, she swam on the far shore, she climbed trees in a part of the forest where no boys had touched bark, and doing so Cozy was convinced her daughter was safely out of those woods. True had sense—Cozy's side of the Bliss family was the side that had sense—so why her daughter should suddenly forsake good sense for a dance, for a man, for a man she knew was her cousin, made no sense to Cozy, it only incensed Cozy, it gave her illest humor license to sully the air in the house with a sulfuric rage. No daughter of hers was going to fall victim fall prey fall in love with an apple from the same tree, not again, if she had to poison it so be it she'd do it, the blood in town was so thin already it wouldn't take much to slip bitter in. Upstairs a pink velvet ribbon was threading through a braid and the braid was coiling a head in a crown draping over a slender shoulder hugging a slightly sloping spine to tie its owner to a suitor who didn't suit her who shouldn't suit her who mustn't suit her. Cozy never told her exactly why.

Everyone had laughed and whispered and counted on whatever fingers they had the years it had taken for Cozy and Remedial to multiply; it was Remedial's thirst for hard cider that threw cold water where heat needed to seep, it was Cozy's hard shell that kept her husband from plunder, it was the cycle of the moon, it was too much chervil, it was everything a small mind in a small town can tell itself when it doesn't want to know itself know the truth—no one knew for certain, but it was surmised that Remedial was not True's father, it was surmised that True's real father was Remedial's best friend, Remedial's best friend as everyone knew was Bull Engersol, and Bull Engersol was Mawz Engersol's father, and if the rumor that had always run through town like a stink of sulfur was true, Mawz was coming to woo his own half sister and neither knew it.

True was upstairs with a pink velvet ribbon and a misconception. A young man was coming to squire her to a dance, a young man whose nervous tic she mistook for a wink, a young man she winked back at and made all his world turn violet. She had known Mawz since he was born, she was born before he was, she was a rose already when he was but a bud, she had always sensed in him a kinship that went beyond the schoolyard, it was barnyard from an early age, though neither understood the attraction. She'd watched the change in him from boy to man, she'd seen how much stronger it made him on horseback, how his snug fit in the saddle was a sight to rein in. Their fathers had been best friends first and cousins second, they fished and horseshoed and hijinxed together, Bull gave Remedial his first slug of cider, it hooked him like a trout. If Remedial needed an extra hand to pull a stump, to roll a rock, to seed a row, Bull was always the pal he could count on to do what needed to be done if he wasn't up to it. It was Bull who found Remedial after True was born, face down in Grunts Pond, cold as a stone, his last bender laid him flat. After that, Bull looked out for True like a father would—from a distance. No wonder. Even before their friendship, Engersols and Blisses had cut up the earth and dribbled their seedlings for as many generations as corn has kernels (what family in town hadn't farmed the same lands together?), but a girl likes a boy because he's a boy she likes, whosoever farmed with whom is irrelevant, he had one eye blue and one eye brown and that's all she needed to see. She liked his eyes; they were crossed, but kind. And they liked her; she loved that. She was Cozy's daughter, sensible as a dollar in most matters, but on this one point she wouldn't make change: if she danced well with Mawz Engersol, she'd marry him.

8: JUBILEE

JUBILEE WAS GOOD with a needle and thread, a stitch in time ticked her hours away. With her brother growing hard as iron and his seams shredding faster than worms could spin silk, it was her job to mend and patch and baste and darn the few clothes he owned and out-wore. Carnival would come home from a day of chopping, all wet and steaming from his ax on up, his shoulder caps splitting open his long johns like foals being born. She'd have him strip down outdoors on the porch, and she'd look the other way as he peeled off every last bit of the reeking tatters and dropped them by her feet. Every day that same pile, the night's mending, and every time Carnival standing in front of his sister full fancy, not ashamed and going nowhere. It was a ritual begun as children and it matured to an adult place that neither needed to speak of, but Jubilee knew it pleased her brother when she'd turn around and look.

She turned somersaults to return the favor. Every Tuesday, from first melt to first freeze, as a member of the Ladies' Tumbling Club. On the small rise of pasture above Grunts Pond, every girl in town letting herself go for an hour of her life. End over end, forwards and backwards and sideways, from seated, from standing, tucking their knock-knees as their feet flew over their faces and opened the petals of their skirts. Jubilee and True and Frainey and Zebeliah, and Petie and Loma, and Onesie and Twosie and Threesie, and Knotsy—all of them, in unison, in pairs, one after another, like a cluster of pinwheels in the high summer grasses, turning turning turning. And the boys in town would watch as the petals peeled to dainties, lying on their stomachs so their pleasure wouldn't show as the girls tumbled to them and tumbled away and their dainties fluttered and whispered, each flip a glimpse of the forbidden, and sometimes, just for Carnival's sake, a bit more.

Russet and Circe were themselves no strangers to the attractions of familiar flesh, but the heat they saw rising between their son and his sister was unsettling even for first cousins. Circe insisted that Jubilee offer her sewing skills to the other families in town, to cousins first, second, any—to stitch her time among more suitable suitors. Someone too smart or not smart enough, someone related but not too related, a shallow pool, yes, but too shallow? (It seemed to be.) On the side too smart there was Kennesaw Belvedere in a crown of laurels and a toga edged in gold, standing on a Corinthian plinth and glowing alabaster. He was the suitor every family sought and his indifference to all who sought him made him all the more attractive, and the more attractive he was the more indifferent he'd become. Kennesaw was exacting with his hems and inseams; he liked his pockets darted and his buttonholes bound. Jubilee's work was tidy, but her loose whip stitches on Carnival's ever-busting britches showed a lack of finesse that fell short, and Kennesaw was not above pointing out that had she taken the care to feather-stitch, the tighter zigzag would keep her brother in his pants, you'd think she'd want that. Still, Kennesaw had mending and Jubilee had skills and Russet and Circe had hopes for this more fitting union. The alternative suitor, on the end not smart enough but appropriate enough, was the Minton with the biggest sniffer of all, Hinkley's son Hunko. Hunko didn't know a featherstitch from a fishhook and didn't care if his seams split or his hems frayed, but he knew enough to demand that Jubilee do for him what she did for Kennesaw because what mattered to Kennesaw mattered to Hunko. Circe instructed Jubilee to ply her needle through Hunko's clothes, too, in case too smart proved too difficult to land, so Jubilee not too happily got out her tools and her spools and whipped up some hems for him, too, darn it. Surely, all this sewing would lead to sowing more seemly and a suitor more suited to their daughter than their son.

But Carnival would have none of it.

He swung his ax for practice as he did for production, it was his labor and his leisure, he kept it with him always and he kept the edge blood sharp, and the closer anyone got to his sister, the sharper that edge sheared. It lay in the grass beside him on the Tuesdays the ladies tumbled, flashing sunlight like a warning beacon as his sister bared her bloomers his way and the other boys knew to keep their distance; it cleaned his fingernails as he watched Hunko watch Kennesaw watch Jubilee tend her mending on their hems and cuffs and inseams especially; it came to the dinner table with him and it made his parents mind their manners when he ate off his sister's plate. Jubilee tumbled and Carnival menaced, she threaded and he dared, she fed his devotion and no one could stop them.

Circe fell to consumption in the winter of the big freeze and, only a few hours after, Russet was ready to be planted in the earth, too. Carnival broke the hard ground himself with a pickax and a mattock, bursting a new section of seam with every swing, and telling himself the stinging in his eyes was sweat and not tears. Six by six he dug the hole to lay his parents side by side. Hunko built a casket for two and Jubilee featherstitched a sock for four to warm their feet forever. Those who attended the small ceremony at Nedewen Field stood shoulder to shoulder in the cold winter air, all eyes on the Aspetucks who would return to a parentless home. Everyone assumed that it was just a matter of time before sister and brother became mother and father.

IT WAS TRUE BLISS who looked around at all the double-joints and wall-eyes and cousin-upon-cousin couplings standing graveside and realized *enough*; who tried to sniff out the air between family genes and when she found little breathing room left anywhere thought *don't*; who took stock of every family trait present in just about every family's offspring of her generation staring into the pit where Russet and Circe lay cousin to cousin and pounded her Drell fist on her Minton palm and said, *Stop, this has to stop, this stops with us!*

True was first born of us all and laid down the law mother may I, and who was to argue when Bliss eyes looked back at Bliss eyes even though your name was Aspetuck or Buckett or O'ums? It was an argument as old as the original drop of water. Whether you believe in miracles or monkeys, we're all cousins first and foremost, diving into the great tide as it goes out to the vast ocean of human expansion. But better that tide going out and dispersing the bloodlines was True's point than riding the one coming in and funneling through a narrow inlet to our secluded pool where every amoeba you meet is divisible by you. Jubilee was certain in her heart that True's theory had as much sense to it as crop rotations, and as she observed her brother and the growing split in his seat as he shoveled the last clods of dirt on the box where the last two cousins to couple lay together she knew enough to nod back at True in silent agreement.

IN A SMALL TOWN there are only so many options for love. The first families who made their way by foot and wagon to this sheltered swath of land were strangers selected at random by whatever magnetic forces pulled them here. Some came coupled already, a child or two in tow, a baby girl in swaddling, a son soon to be born, but more arrived alone with nothing but their name and an unnamed beating in their hearts of what they could make of tomorrow.

You set sail for some new life and see ahead a distant shore and you are sure in your youthful zeal that you are the first to see it, and you can smell its earthy air beckoning to you across the waves, and in its thrall you need no sextant to guide your ship to its port. You bust up the earth there and clear a field for growing, you fell trees and hew them and build a house by hand, you want to make use of the time you have here and so you look to each other for warmth. A Bliss marries a Minton marries a Buckett marries a Drell, and as your world expands you have every expectation of new bloodlines staking their claims in neighborly fashion and new opportunities for romance and sure enough they come. Now a Swampscott for a Minton and an O'ums for a Bliss, soon a Saflutis meets a Buckett and a Drell a Belvedere. But comes a day when Engersols and Hurlbutts and Hackensack/Whiskerhoovens run out of Aspetucks and Soyles, and the new additions in town trickle to a Trousard, then an Upland, and at the very last, a Lope. One morning you wake up and there are no more new neighbors to come, and the small town of options you thought would grow and grow starts to shrink and shrink, bringing you back to a Bliss marrying a Minton marrying a Buckett marrying a Drell marrying a Bliss marrying a Minton marrying a Buckett marrying a Drell. Eyes cross, joints double, wombs go barren, newborns pass. Cousins run out of cousins. And what's left is Aspetuck on Aspetuck or nothing. No love. Cold feet forever.

True's admonishment was as sensible as heavy wool socks. If Jubilee knew what was good for her, she'd knit herself a pair right quick. Then again, she could go the way of Frainey Swampscott, down a path as ancient as the first dalliance, but that was a different animal altogether, from which there would be no turning back.

9: FRAINEY

SOME THINGS COME NATURAL, some you force. Growing up happens on its own, growing old, mourning, remembering. Doings most are not naturally apt at: adjusting to the unexpected, pretending it doesn't matter, forgiving it.

Frainey Swampscott was between a child and the early-early budding of being a woman when both her parents succumbed to the big fever the spring of the first big fever. The fever snuck into town after sunset on a day when the air was in no rush to move about and the smell of pork stew lingered long after the fat congealed on the remains, and before the moon went to sleep that next

daybreak the fever settled a crowd on St. Peter's stoop
of Porcine Belvedere, Etingem Saflutis, Hephelonious
Soyle, Brisket Whiskerhooven, poor kid right in his
prime, that horse's ass Boyle Lope, and Frainey's mother and father as if they were a go-together like biscuits
and butter and were taken off the table as one.

Frainey's mother came into this world a Buckett, her
name was Salomee in honor of a woman some man lost
his head over, she had Drell in her and Engersol and
Bliss and Minton, too. Frainey's granddaddy had lost
his heart to a first wife who never made it through child-
birth and took the child with her, and because his new
wife and child almost did the same thing and the fear
of losing both again scared him from wishing on the
future, he made the child a remembrance of what had
been and named him Wuzz. The night her parents took
ill Frainey was asleep in front of an open window in the
small rear room off the stairs on the upper half floor of
her family's story-and-a-half saltbox and her parents
were in the room directly below with the windows
closed and the door shut and not so much as a crack in
the lath letting in air. The fever, which she later learned
had meandered across the valley with no more purpose
to its travels than a stroll on a lovely night, stopped first
at the Saflutises', then the Whiskerhoovens', caught a
current across Grunts Pond to the Lopes', leaped over
the ridge to the Soyles', and might have followed a

straight line through the woods to the edge of town with a brief how-do-you-do at the Belvederes' before evanescing into the far-away, but it didn't; instead, it first detoured fully around the Minton homestead and grazed the O'umses'—Knotsy came down with a mighty case of the snots—and then laid siege on the Swampscott saltbox like that had been its sole intended target all along. Frainey, maybe named after a birdcall, maybe not, slept angelically, deep in dream about an escapade with her pet goat, Chippewa. As they romped in a forever world, two kids side by side, the fever breezed through Frainey's open window and over her sleeping body and slipped down the stairs and under the door into the sealed off bedroom where Salomee and Wuzz slumbered, and without waking either, dove head first into Salomee's nose and Wuzz's open mouth and went to work.

A fever on a breeze is a random thing; it can blow this way or that and take hold here or wherever. It can blow through an open window and over the sleeping body of a child and leave her be like a pie cooling on the sill, and instead make a nuisance of itself down in a part of a house where no breeze was meant to meander. A fever, unlike a name, doesn't have to remind you of anything other than itself. It's a bad deed done once and gone. What it leaves behind, the effect of it, that's the part of it that lingers, that's the real story, perpetual and life-lasting. Random and done-and-gone is a fever blowing into town late one night and out of all the pairs of parents asleep in their beds it picking Frainey's parents to take in a single breath. The story, the one Frainey has never been able to untell herself, the perpetual part, is how a daughter who was already sisterless and brotherless was made motherless and fatherless before sunup, and who became an animal almost overnight and almost stayed that way for life.

PEOPLE STAND AROUND FRESH HOLES in the ground and do what sheep do. They look down in the hole, down on the box in it, curiously, as if there might be something down there to eat, then they glance over at the mounded dirt that came out of the hole and will go back on top of the box. A chill wind ripples by and they shiver a bit and pull their fleece linings tight, they hear a tree limb crack and fall on a bed of forest moss not too far off and they look around to try and see where, they turn their attention back to the hole in the ground and the box in it and they stare awhile, and while they do, they do what they were too sheepish to do at first, they think about themselves.

Not a tear was shed for Etingem Saflutis, not by Agapanthus, she was cold and wanted to get back home to her lap rug and her cats. Petie and Loma Soyle dropped a few drips in the dirt in earnest near the hole where Hephelonious lay—Petie for the petty treatment her sister would surely now give her with their mother now gone, Loma for the smaller percentage of affection that she received from their mother compared to what her sister basked in, but now that it was gone with the box in the hole it came to her: it was better than none. Kennesaw's bluer-than-blues weren't gunked up or watery at all; you could see it in his eyes and in the clenched set of his cleft and chisel it was delayed justice to take Porcine at last, after all she hadn't protected him from. He almost buried her with his father's belt, that strip of an unjust god, but that was going too far. Mola Whiskerhooven shook her head with the regret that her son would no longer pepper her mashed potatoes with tadpoles, she'd grown to like the taste, and Hunko Minton was glad his own eyes weren't set so far apart on his face like his friend Brisket's were that when he blinked his ears wiggled, and around the hole and even now all these years since, some of us still blush recalling Brisket's lisp echoing in the darkness that warm still night in his first squirting days when he was down on the rocky shores of Grunts Pond and grunted out "*Knotsthy*!" like a flick of thunder. His loss is a living thing. As to that horse's ass Boyle Lope—the best his litter of daughters could say of the loss of him was *oh well* and *there you have it* and *'bout time!*

Awe more than anything might have been granted
to the double departing of Salomee and Wuzz. Since
neither had been all that special on their own at least
going out together was an occasion. But Frainey did not
strike us as all that sad-hearted that her parents were in
a hole and gone for good. She was restless by that hole.
Sucking in air and hissing it out. Rocking on her heels.
Mad and impatient, as though someone had done her a
wrong and was taking their sweet time making it right.
True placed a tender hand on Frainey's shoulder to con-
sole her friend but the girl exploded from her reach like
a frog you don't see till it jumps. She had brought with
her Chippewa and it was Chippewa she turned to for
whatever comfort she'd allow—stroking the goat's neck,
its beard, holding onto a horn. The only sign she gave
that something pulled at her heart was when she pulled
Chippewa's rope tight when the goat tried to nibble on
her mother's box as it was lowered into its hole.

Around a graveyard there are the usual politics of
grief: who stands nearest the next and dearest, who
kicks in the first clod of dirt, who's happiest that the
body in the box isn't theirs. So important at the time are
such logistics; later on, the simplest facts survive. Holes
were dug. Passages read. It was cold for May. Chippewa
dunged. Everyone for the most part went back to their
homes and resumed their chores and their grievanc-
es and their lives; True wanted Frainey to come home

with her to stay, the goat they'd make a place for later, but Frainey mulishly said no. Her parents weren't really gone-gone, she told herself. They were away-gone, off somewhere, not that she knew the difference, not that they'd ever gone off somewhere without her, not that anyone she'd ever known of had gone off somewhere never to return, though there was a rumor about Kennesaw, yet here he was, and, so, too, could her parents be: they were away-gone but they'd be back, they weren't really in that hole, they were at home, waiting for her, that's where they were. She had found them stiff and cold, she had run to town for help to rouse them, later when they were carted off and she was shooed to True's, she knew something bad had happened like when lightning struck and the whole house shook, then the shaking stopped and all was back to normal, so all would be back to normal, they'd be back like nothing had struck, she was sure of it. True's concern trailed after Frainey and the goat as they left the boneyard for their long walk back to who-knows-what. Few others gave a second thought to the who-knows-what that would become of the orphan and her goat.

THE GRAVESIDE GATHERING had started at noon and was over by half-past (why linger when what's done is done?), and it took most of the rest of the day for

Frainey and Chippewa to make it back home. The goat was grazing on rogue grass and garlic and spring asparagus and she didn't like to eat in a hurry. At home a few chickens skittered about on the front porch, and some of the cracks in the floorboards were sprouting a gash of moss green with a touch of gold in it like they had an infection. Frainey went in the house expecting to find her mother by the cookstove skimming fat off the pork roast and boiling water and pushing the hair off her face with her forearm and it falling back like it always did, but the only life in there was a fly circling the cold stew pot. If Papa was anywhere he was in the barn, in the back stall behind Chippewa's stall, where he kept the big wooden trunk with the lock that was always locked. It had belonged to Wuzz's father. Frainey knew where he hid the key to that lock. He never carried it on him unless he was away from home for longer than a morning, and when she looked for it and expected to not find it because she was certain he and Mama were away-gone and would be back before dark she found it hanging from its peg on a beam and something in her seized. What had made her mad before made her scared now; could away-gone and gone-gone be the same thing?

No explaining why you sometimes do things because they just feel right, like your hands know a secret they haven't told your head. Frainey took that feeling that seized her in the barn right into the house and over to the stuck shut window in the downstairs bedroom where Wuzz and Salomee once slumbered. She couldn't get the upper sash down with her fingertips or the lower to lift up with the butts of her palms so she bashed it with her father's bootjack and shattered every pane. The air allowed in hit her face like a slapped hand. Any stray breeze with a demon on its breath would now blow through that room and spare its occupants of any further fevers—that's what happened in hers. All hands and no head, Frainey next lay down a carpet of straw over every exposed inch of floor in the room and even on the bed, and dragged in a tin tub that her mother had used for washing and filled it with fresh water, and from that mourning day on, Chippewa never spent another night out in the barn.

Frainey tried spooning her small body against Chippewa's that night to feed off her warmth, but Chippewa flicked and twitched in her sleep and every time she shook with a goat dream a horn jabbed Frainey, so Frainey gave over the bed to Chippewa and curled into a ball on the straw floor beside it.

It didn't take long for Chippewa to take to her new surroundings and her place in them. She had full run of the house, ground level and half upper, and Frainey let her do whatever she liked. What she liked was to sashay from room to room grazing, tasting and spitting out bits of this 'n' that (sash weight, saucer, settee), depositing her doings here and there, giving up her milk to Frainey now and then. Chippewa took to staying in not only on wet mornings, but on cold mornings, too, and hot mornings, then it was all mornings, and eventually all days and every day became like that first day with Frainey out foraging foliage and toting fresh water and she learned to hopscotch the growing mounds of pungent dung and swat her way through the flies that settled in that hilly territory like early man on the move and made the wooden house hum like a living thing.

The goat was in hog heaven. She had no need to leave the house for any reason at any time. She could eat her fill and empty it, wander, slumber, when and wherever. She was no longer an animal in suffrage to mankind— the animal kingdom had been turned on its crown at last and now goat kept girl. Frainey was her fetch dog and beast of burden all in one, feeding her, grooming her with the hairbrush she no longer used on her own head, balling up in a corner away from Chippewa when the goat wasn't feeling herself. If Frainey had had it in her, she might even have lactated her own sweetness for the goat's daily enjoyment, in fact she took to pulling at her own eensie-teensies in hopes of stimulating their flow.

May flowed into June as Frainey became what she never dreamed humanly possible. From that first day home the rain rained and it didn't let up, and Frainey like she did that first wet day took to her daily habit of dashing out for the daily forage while Chippewa remained inside dry and her needs high priority. Frainey hadn't learned beans about sowing or reaping or frying or baking or mold or maggots or mites. When the little food she had left began to squirm, she took to dining on whatever Chippewa turned up her dented nose at, and when what went in leafy and lush green came out of her mute-green and mossy they were both intrigued. Chippewa was growing rounder and more self-satisfied with every day while Frainey in no time at all gave gaunt a scare. Her belly collapsed like a rotten pumpkin. Her hair fell out in shanks. If the looking glass in the hall hadn't fallen and shattered she might have noticed her eye whites turning raccoon brown and her pink cheeks gone wolf gray.

NOAH HAD COLLECTED TWO of every living thing on earth and bunked them by species so they'd keep to their own kind. He'd been around the sand dunes once or twice himself and knew that some mammals might stray from their own back yards and take up with a reptile next door. These things happen sure as bushes burst into flames and oceans split in two. But such unusually close solicitude between girl and goat was perhaps not what Noah spent all that time afloat for. True said as much the day she came to pay a call on Frainey and was overwhelmed as much by the disquietude that met her eyes as by the stench only Satan himself could belch out.

Frainey had all but given up hopscotching the dung piles and had stopped doing her own doings outdoors, bringing the outhouse in and throughout. The sight and smell of her young friend filthed and numb-glazed in a haze of flies squatting in the front hall of the house over a mound of her own fresh moss was bad enough, but seeing the goat lounging resplendent on what had been the parlor davenport, her bag belly big as a slattern's ransom, lunching on the last of the horse-hair stuffing and giving True the evil bone button eye—to True's orderly stomach, that was the last straw. No, the last straw that broke her stomach was the moving straw, and the walls a-squirm with life.

MAYANS BAKED ADOBE in the hot south sun and slathered on plaster that outlasted them all. True didn't take a trowel to Frainey, just the opposite—the dung and dirt on her was caked solid as a ruin and would take an excavation to remove. A chisel, she'd have used one if it didn't all come off with water and a horse brush and hard scrubbing and more water and more hard scrubbing and a ghost dusting of lye to burn off what water didn't exterminate. Frainey didn't make a sound, her body juddered this way and that with every hard scrub, she was something underwater in a rip tide being pushed and pulled in place. It took almost a full day to unearth the orphan under all that grime and bring her back to a being that didn't smell or look like it lived in a hole.

Forty days was all it had been since Salomee and Wuzz went in the ground and in that time Frainey had descended lower. True figured a mood must have settled on Frainey's skin like a swarm of bees and stung her sadness numb so she could open her eyes and see her way ahead without tears. From there it bored through the barrier of muscle and tissue on every inch of her to saddle every corpuscle in her bloodstream and ride them down the evolutionary trail to a place where bees had tusks. Forty days of suspended floating in an island-sized boat had saved two of everything living in their natural states, each being as recognizable stepping off as the day they boarded. In the same not-so-long length of time, Frainey had shipped out a girl in the early-early of becoming a woman, but left parentless and bereaved and bunked with a beast she called friend, the girl bested the beast in unashamed atavism. True reasoned that, for whatever reason, something in Frainey retreated to a place in her grief where only a beast could show her that wild was better than weeping. If her parents were truly gone-gone, a memory instead of something recognizable, what was to stop Frainey from becoming a memory herself? Sometimes, the hand doesn't know any better than the head, so a child who doesn't know to save her own life will simply ruin it instead.

10: Kennesaw

A SMALL TOWN APPROACHES the doings of its past with a heel on a spade in the dirt, digging up where you set it or leaving set what you'd rather not unearth.

When people want to know your business, in time they make it their business to root in your dirt and come up a fistful. If it's something you have and they want it they'll step hard on that spade and grind their boot heel on its edge for as long as it takes to break the hardest earth to get at it. But if it's something you've done that they've done themselves or want to do, then that spade turns tender tungsten around the tiniest roots and leaves alone what they'd just as soon not have you stir up in them. So, a child gets hit or bit or worse in a house across town, or a dalliance in the shadows produces one man's sprout from another man's seed, or a suffering love that was already secret is snuffed out in secret with no chance to suffer it out in the wide open, or a spooking is blamed for a man gone ghost, or half a dozen more doings the Good Book says are bad get done, get done again, and again, and again, and no one says one word, and more than likely it's happening in more than one house. Time notches its bedpost on comings and doings like these.

As A TOWN DIGS, so does a single man. When the game of Adam and Abel first began, Kennesaw was too young to understand what was happening to him, happening upon him. He thought perhaps that this was as it should be between fathers and sons, he didn't question it or even speak of it, an unspoken voice in him said don't, so he didn't. His reasoning was sound for a boy who followed his father's orders. If you dug a hole in clay, clay is what you'd find and clay, as his father assured him, is as normal as dirt. He had no reason to suspect that if he dug down deeper, there might be clay of a deeper hue, more rust than brown, like dirt mixed with blood. Or, if in another spot entirely he shivved his spade into soil of an exotically different composition such as the mulch of decayed plants, the fistful he'd find would be a version of the story altogether different than the one his father learned him. But if Kennesaw had believed wholeheartedly what his father said, if all clay was indeed as normal as dirt as his father had assured him, he might have traded stories with Carnival or Luddy or Mawz as one would boast openly about a first slug of applejack or a stolen toke on a briar pipe. An open boast would have echoed across Grunts Pond, and had it, a groin-busting *Godourfather!* would have been as often a grunt-out out there as the more common *yeahverily!* and *comeallyefaithful!* and even Brisket Whiskerhooven's nasal, but potent, *Knotsthy!*

Yet, as Kennesaw matured, he sensed that an open boast this was not. Open boasts were Columbine Buckett and Russet Aspetuck and their mutual mooniness over his ax and his long thumb, or the seventy-two hours in an airless shack when Hock Hackensack marinated his new bride Anamana in the ever-funky musk of his skunk loving. Open boasts are titter-makers even a spinster can approve of, they're gasps and giggles straight out of the Good Book chapter and verse that come at you winking like a drunken limerick. Open boasts get passed with the peas at Sunday Sit Down, they're stitched like an old dress hem into a trousseau quilt to inspire the next bed, they're stories the old folks bring out into the night without mosquito netting on them that raise the kind of bumps nearly everyone present is happy for.

A closed boast is a private suffering that everybody knows about yet keeps their hush about. It's a Carnival Aspetuck unable to conceal his celebration of his sister Jubilee. And it's certainly a Flummox raising Cain on Kennesaw in the game of Adam and Abel. A closed boast is right there on the table next to the peas at Sunday Sit Down, a mouth-watering temptation in a ladle-less china tureen that everyone seated has the phantom taste of on their tongue, but unlike the peas swimming in the butter of acceptability, not a one will risk asking for it to be passed. A closed boast is too close to the bone of human weakness, the raw matter of lust in unfettered free-for-all that courses deep and concealed within us all.

A closed boast is a Hunko Minton, clandestine and pulsing behind a pond-side boulder, with his boyish love down around his ankles and his mannish heart in both hands, pining for Kennesaw, pining, pining. A boast more closed, so closed it had no name, was a Kennesaw and his own ongoing indulgence of Hunko's clandestine curiosity down on that rocky shore of Grunts Pond, and his own clandestine curiosity about that curiosity that kept him coming back for more. Add to that the matter of clay, shovels full of it on a daily basis. With his father, the clay had an unexpectedly earthy air: there was a light dusting of pleasure in the uncertain doings for Kennesaw—a pleasure that he wished he could resist but couldn't. It was to his relief, though, that the pleasure reached a quick, violent peak, and like an air-borne scent, dissipated just as soon as his father let him go. The curiosity with Hunko, however, was as different as a cyclone is to a sigh. That pleasure for Kennesaw wasn't a dusting, that pleasure was a hole-filler, and as uncertain as he was about the air he shared with his father, his doings with Hunko blew onto him a pleasure that long clung to him like Hock Hackensack's stink. And, oh how he wished he didn't so completely enjoy that smell.

THE HEEL ON THE SPADE can only sink the spade so deep. Kennesaw's father said clay was as normal as dirt, yet no one else ever iterated that aphorism at Sunday Sit Down, nor stitched it into a quilt, nor grunted it under the stars. A grunt here, a grunt there, a chorus of grunts in the moonlight air as far as Kennesaw could tell were not about clay at all—they were about pink velvet ribbons and skirts tumbled high and the farm-fresh smell of a girl's slightly dirty wrist as she passed you the peas.

Why Kennesaw refused entry to any possibility that there were others who staked the same claim to clay is as big a riddle as those cobra-headed colossi along the Euphrates. After all, right in front of his own nose was clay of the purest form. It was clay that didn't parade itself as dirt, didn't even try to sell you on any comparison at all, it just dropped its pants and said to the world: I'm clay—want to get dirty?

The nakedness of a Hunko of clay both thrilled Kennesaw and unsettled him. The beaming willingness of the boy to wait out his own maturation until it could swim itself upstream, and then present the bounty of himself to Kennesaw as he would a cupped palmful of tadpoles fresh from the first spring run-off, was the single most nakedly pure act of humanity that Kennesaw had ever experienced. There on the pond shore for all the fluidity they shared until Kennesaw closed the tap of his heart, their daily play was everything his father's game of Adam and Abel wasn't. Now it was Kennesaw who was the older one, the larger one, the one more into his manhood. He could bend the rules of their play, bind them with his own belt to a post if it so disposed him, whenever he so wanted, and more to the point, if. He, Kennesaw, could take from Hunko as Flummox took from him, exert a captor's power over his pulsing young admirer as his father did over him; take the boy, spend him, and always keep the boy guessing as to the next opportune moment he'd be able to get at him again.

But Kennesaw wasn't Flummox, and in Hunko he did not see what his father saw in him, whatever it was that his father saw in him. With Hunko, Kennesaw was one—a pound of iron on a farrier's scale, no better, no bigger; ounce for ounce, no different than a pound of feathers. This little stub was his equal in ardor, if not in measure, and the delight they simultaneously showered upon one another should have been enough to overflow a china tureen for a lifetime of Sunday Sit Downs. Hunko happily would have been the bowl to Kennesaw's ladle for the pleasure of a table ever set for two. He by himself would build them a foundation of clay by hand, build walls of clay, a roof of clay, and in such the solid structure clay would be as normal as clay and whoever did not like it could eat their own dirt. But it was Kennesaw, with his heel on the spade and the spade digging, digging, at some layer deep down who one day wouldn't dig any deeper; he hit a rock or a root, and he left the shovel stuck there, and left Hunko stuck there, too.

FATHERS. THESE MEN WHOSE BIOLOGY turns them brute and who repent for nothing—why does our blood compel us to love them? In the privacy of their individual confusions, Kennesaw and True asked of themselves this same question for the many remaining years of their lives, and for the many remaining years of their lives conclusions eluded them.

Kennesaw let slip his uncertainty to her one afternoon, one winter's day one foot at a time on brittle
ice. He hadn't called it a name yet, in his heart it did
not answer to "shame," but in his head—happy as he
was—the moniker stuck, and stuck as sharp as a spade's
honed edge. He couldn't align his bluer-than-blues on
True's browns when he told her what was happening
in his own home, no more so than he could look her in
the browns when he told her what was happiness on the
shore's edge. But her browns had a way of piercing his
blues with an honesty as sure as her name. She told him
a story that she had heard at a Sunday Sit Down not too
long after Mawz Engersol had been turned out, and Bull
Engersol had been turned under, and her mother Cozy
had turned her own disenchantment with life into a de-
canter of sweet venom from which she filled her glass
nightly until she was ready to turn in.

That Flummox, Cozy said between heaving gulps,
*like father, like son. His old man, Congress, was bad weather
blowing south, and that Flummox turns his weathervane the
same direction, too. I'd watch out for that Kennesaw if he ever
has a son.*

To Kennesaw, True uttered this rebuttal: *you're no
more Flummox than Hunko is you,* she told him, and although her words reeked of logic and clarity, Kennesaw
nearly puked from confusion. That one thing could be
two things was not a plateau of reason Kennesaw had

ever himself ascended to. The result was a teeter-totter of mind and heart, one up, one down, one down, one up, with his life, he felt, hinged on a swivel.

KENNESAW NEVER FIGURED need to watch out for what old winds blew. It was hard to imagine any other son in town set upon by the man who begot him, but here it was in his own family, a closed boast with its own history of shame. How far back a hush was kept is another poser for those cobra-headed colossi. Here was his father, Flummox, doing to his son, Kennesaw, what he knew to do because it was done to him. And here was his father, Congress, doing to his son, Flummox, what he knew to do no doubt because it was done to him. And here's his father, Plato, no doubt doing to his son, Congress, what he knew to do because it was no doubt done to him . . . a closed boast that, for all Kennesaw knew, went all the way back to Noah, to Lamech, to Methuselah, to Enoch, to Cain, to Adam, to clay, to air.

If clay was as normal as dirt, was clay as normal as clay as Hunko would have him believe? Was there no relationship to dirt at all? Was what existed between him and Hunko as different from his doings with his father as clay is from mulch? Was there such a finely tilled soil where good and bad could grow from the same seed? He had wanted to believe it. Hunko had pressed him to believe it. Even True in her own brown-eyed honesty had given him the wink of her approval. Believe it. But he couldn't. Hunko was like a son to him. And if Hunko was like a son, what did that make him?

Delight too often is turned soil that loses its sweetness if nothing is planted in it to grow. From seeing his young stub as his equal to seeing himself as the lad's abuser was all in a day's plowing. Kennesaw turned his back on clay then and there. Shut himself off from dirt, too. Scraped his heels clean of anything that might cling.

11: TRUE

TRUE WAS UPSTAIRS with a pink velvet ribbon that would weave a veil of white and a lilt in her throat humming love songs. Cozy was downstairs in a snit that her daughter was in a pet about a half-brother she thought was a cousin. And Mawz? He was coming up the walk coming up the steps stepping to the front door to call on a girl with an abundance of jack-in-the-pulpits he had picked for her, his arms overflowing with pinks and purples bowing shyly in their sheaths of green, he would give them to her and she would love him for them and they would dance and they would wed and they would bed.

Cozy's fury opened the vestibule door before Mawz had a chance to tap on the opaque glass (and before he even withdrew his knocking knuckle), her heat was enough to blast his blue eye brown and his brown eye straight. She said to him in a killing whisper, *You're not going to see her, stay away from her,* and she gave him a moment to let the threat absorb. He had a smile on his face that was a fresh peach turning, and as soon as the fuzz of him darkened, she drew her knife to peel the spoiling skin. *Ask your father,* she said, *if he hasn't already told you,* she hissed, *it's time that he told you,* she said, *the rumor is true.*

If Mawz was in a saddle, say, and the horse stopped abruptly, his body would continue forward an extra split second and then the pommel would crotch him. A split second before he was a boy with an armful of flowers for a girl he was taking to a dance and a split second later still in motion he was on the threshold of not breathing, ever again. The jack-in-the-pulpits in his arm were all the sweeter to Cozy in their wasted, wilting way. *Leave now,* she told him then, stealing the air and taking it back inside behind the closing door. What Mawz did on the other side of that opaque glass Cozy wasn't concerned with. She was waiting now for her daughter to come downstairs, her sensible daughter who needed to come to her senses where boys were concerned.

True bounded down the stairs two at a hop, her braid

with its pink velvet ribbon clippety-clop on her back. She hadn't heard the door, the exchange, the air sucking into a void; it was the double ting-ting of the clock's 8:15 that brought her excitement down to ground level. *He's late,* she said to her mother, and Cozy shook her head in mute *oh well.* True got herself a glass of water, she smoothed her braid over her right shoulder then her left, she sat down, she stood up, she pulled back the lace curtain on the parlor's front oriel and peered out to the gate for a sign in the dark. She perched on the edge of a hassock and smoothed her skirt and smoothed it again. Cozy took up her knitting on the davenport in silence; the only commentary she'd let loose was the click of her needles. She could see on True's face, around her mouth, around her eyes, what True had seen in the looking glass upstairs when she allowed herself that bit of annoyance: the tight skin, the pinch of disappointment—men do that to a woman's face, Cozy's smile seemed to say. The clock's ting-tong said it was 8:30 and ting-ting at 8:45 and nine times tong-tong it was nine.

Was it a ghost, a riff of effluvium in the breeze, a moth against the opaque glass of the front vestibule door that caught True's attention at that moment and said to her go to the door, girl, your boy's been here? Whatever came over her, her sensible self knew to obey, and to Cozy's silent thrill True flew to the front vestibule door and rattled its opaque glass as she pulled it open in a rush. There was no one there, there was no air, no moth, no Mawz, nothing to grab hold of in the dark, nothing she thought, until she looked down at her feet and saw a mound of jack-in-the-pulpits on the porch, he had dropped them in a heap, a heap as high as her boots, and they were curling in the summer night, hundreds of them, rotting to slime. So, True slammed the door shut. She slammed it shut for good. Cozy never said a word. And True was left to hate the only boy she might have loved.

12: CARNIVAL

TAKE AN AX AND CHOP HIS LIFE into two uneven stacks: the years of split britches and the years when it all fell loose.

In his split britches years, everything about him was bursting. His strength and his sweat, his shoulder caps and slab back and thighs, the robustness of his youth and axmanship that he wasn't ashamed to show. Unabashed of all, the burst he wouldn't keep down for manners or modesty, was the thrust of his feelings for Jubilee. In another town with another girl—or a cow or a goat or a horse—Carnival would be the stallion to lay your bets on, who'd fill every stall and paddock and crib with the abundance swelling inside him. That his nostrils happened to flare for his own sister—you don't need a talk-to about animal husbandry to know what that's about. The scent was in the air and the air was at home.

People whispered. Some, like True, frowned out loud and often. Mawz, more than anyone, had a real sense of brotherhood with Carnival, inadvertent as it was, and having suffered for it, was much against it.

With their parents in their box and their box in the ground, the flirting accelerated unfettered. Jubilee swatted away Carnival's attentions with a tut-tut and a blush, yet when his hot blood climbed the Fahrenheits, her hands stopped being so prissy. To say that makes her sound like a temptress, which no one ever accused her of being. Her high bust sat high with no boning to boost it and her knees knocked on their own and her cowlick and her long thumbs and her buckteeth were as the good Lord saw fit to outfit her with. She had what she had and what she did with it she'd have done, brother or no. She wasn't one to get all girly and gussy for any other, and surely not for a brother, but if, through no efforts on her part, built-in girlishness and guss happened to draw the slobber out of a male who just happened to be her brother, there must have been sound reasoning in the divine plan or why would He have made her enticements so tempting?

She wasn't one to take it to town, nor one to hide it in a tin on a top shelf in a pantry. She went about her ways the way she did day after day, and if things stirred, things stirred. She watched her brother strip down at the end of every day on the back porch and pile his mendables before her. She stooped to pick them up, took a peek, turned to go, gandered back for anything overlooked, looked again, then got gone to get down to her sewing. That was just the way it was.

Every night pieced together like this: she sat in the corner chair between the woodstove and the window, framed in a moody glow by the day's waning light and the night's fire building. She'd position her heck box in front of her with her knock-knees locking it in place. She'd mound her brother's mendables in her lap, they were often still steaming with the smell of him, and always she'd arrange them to have the rear split facing up to fix first. She'd pull a bobbin from her box, a different color for each waiting tear—brown for a shoulder, blue for the rear, red for the rest. She'd unspool a length of blue thread long enough to double and bind, and when she had it, she'd pull it broken with a mighty snap. She'd examine both ends of thread to determine which end was less the ragged for threading, then put the better end in her mouth and run her tongue around it to lick it smooth, and slowly pull it out and grind her buckteeth down on it and chew it fine for feeding. She'd pluck a needle from a red felt ball of nothing but needles and eye its eye for the opening it would yield. She'd pinch the needle between two fingers and steady it for the piercing. And then that fine thread end she'd slip through the eye like nothing else mattered, let go of it and regrip it on the other side and pull it all the way through as long as she wanted it until she was ready to stop and tie the knot.

The process had such delicateness to it that Carnival could barely contain himself. His days were big broad swings of a big broad ax blade gashing and gouging and ravaging the land. Huge trunks fell to his rhythms, and logs rolled over and took his hacking swings. Thick wood chips and splinters long as silverware mounded at his feet, chip dust clouded the air around him and wood shards stuck sweated to his skin, and no one took notice. It was all muscle in motion, nothing thoughtful to it, no refined precision, just swing and hack and swing and hack, and sweat and split and hurry home. And here she was with delicate fingers doing delicate deeds for him, the only moistness about her on the tip of her licking tongue, and her attentions so focused on that thread feeding into that needle's eye that he ached to throw over his own labors for hers and be that thread between her fingers feeding into that needle's eye.

He'd watch her stitch: under and out and over and

in, and under and out and over and in. His heart was pulled in with every plunge of her needle, and every time the tip of it came back up the veins in his bulky neck pulsed with longing. He could watch her sew for hours; he could go all night.

Some nights she used a thimble; some nights her finger went bare. The decision to cap came from the rent mendables themselves: were the day's splits the same old tear along the same old line, or did her brother burst a new seam in a way she'd need to learn? New splits always were tougher to master; they always tore along the edge of a double-dart that seemed indestructible but wasn't. She had to press down harder on the needle to plunge it in to doubled-fabric, and brace it firmer to push it back up. It led to a kind of unwieldiness of action—the struggle to force the needle through had the potential to do harm, maybe cause a new tear, maybe prick skin and draw blood. Sometimes, she misjudged the night's needs, went unprotected when she should have shown more care. Those were the nights when she was too far along in the rhythm of her stitches to stop and thimble up, when her own motions of stitch and plunge were as coarse as her brother's hack and swing. Carnival hoped it was the mending she liked best. Her whole body on these nights was engaged in the struggle. Her knock-knees clamped the heck box tighter between them. Her high bust heaved higher with every forced under and out and over and in. The tip of her tongue oozed out of her mouth and seeped over her buckteeth like hot fruit from a piecrust. She even sweated. Once she burst a seam of her own and Carnival nearly exploded.

A bit of blood could always feed him, but more than a bit made him queasy. On the night when she stuck herself and the stick struck a gusher, and the blood seeped down the needle and flushed across the fabric she was mending, she dropped both needle and mendable with a moan and shoved the finger under her buckteeth and deep in her mouth and sucked the blood as though there'd be no more of it if she didn't. She watched her brother watch her suck her life back into herself, and when she heard his heavy breathing catch and shift from animal to anxious she knew that what had ruptured could never be repaired. The sight of all that thick rich blood spilled on his pant split— spilled for him—drew the air from his lungs and the blood from his head. He had to sit fast and rest when it happened. It was the first time he made his sister bleed this way. She felt the pain, but he was the one who cried.

IN ANOTHER TOWN with another man, Jubilee wouldn't have sewn so openly. She would have kept her needles and bobbins latched in a box in a room with a door with a lock. She'd have moved her chair from the corner to a place where shadows couldn't flicker, where the day outside and the night within had no opportunity for such a sultry intersect. She'd have chosen a mendable at random and a thread color by chance and thimbled up no matter what. In another town with another man she would have been a seamstress by day and, if night, out of sight if sewing. Her sweating, heaving struggles with needles through double-darts would have been her most private moments, never shared with any, and if she drew blood, she'd have the sense to seek comfort in a bandage, or barring that, suck her own life in private, in a room with a door with a lock, never in the flickers, never before her brother. There's such a thing as carrying a point too far.

Once her skin bore his wounds, there would be no other town, no other man, not that there would have been otherwise, but still. She still tended the occasional mending for Kennesaw, whose fuss had nothing to do with her flesh, and Hunko, whose interest in flesh was not about drawing blood from it. Other girls in town could sew well enough, mend a shoulder, fix a split, but none had ever effectuated a darn that elicited from any man such a *hot damn*. Jubilee looked different, walked different, sewed like she was sewing not for herself, not even for her brother, but sewing for something that might outlast them both; it was not that long after their parents went into the ground, and she was flush with whatever it was. It was in her cheeks, it was in her ankles, and by the next full moon it was in the seams of her clothes that slowly started to burst.

A DOG WHO'S DONE WRONG will hug the ground around you as he dares to come closer with the hope you'll forgive him. Carnival returned each night from his daily hewing and splitting and stripped off his mendables as he always had before, and stood before his sister full fancy as he always had before, but unlike he always had before, he no longer swelled with pride in her presence, because, unlike she always had before, Jubilee no longer looked. The nightly dress down, which had been Carnival's earthiest pleasure of the day, was now a stray dog at his sister's back door, and where she had once indulged him with succor she now closed the door on him and left the hound dog hanging.

But a rebuff is no redress when the dog has already been fed. She could turn her back on Carnival, avert her eyes, leave a room when he entered, wake before him and go to sleep after, but it would not alter the face of the facts. Sister had allowed brother what brother had been drooling for for a dog's age. He had hungered for it and it had happened, and the very thing wagging tongues had warned about had happened, too. Embarrassed before each other, they could sidestep what was growing; she could scold him with her silence and he could whimper in penance, and in each one's lone remove from the truth they could tell themselves any lie they wanted. But there was a town to encounter. A town that had not seen a lump bigger than a day's loaf of bread rise in any home since the last of their parents had delivered the last of their friends.

Among them Jubilee would have the harder time explaining things. By the second full moon her seams were starting to burst in ways she could not mend with a simple stitch and a self-effacement. (Was she indulging in too many fritters? Fat chance.) There'd be quizzical titters, and titters would become tuts, and tuts would yield snorts, and snorts would step behind barns and cluster in snickers and then gang up in sneers. It would be thought: cousins had cousined and look around at the peculiarities that had wrought. It would be said: surely this kind of close encounter would bring to bear something even a dog would turn away from. It would be certain, Jubilee felt in her gut, that the derision would be all but unlivable. She circled around a conclusion like it was a bowl of unfamiliar scraps and finally dug her nose in and chewed and swallowed the only foreseeable way to sidestep the trouble. She and Carnival would have to go. They'd have to leave New Eden.

JUBILEE GATHERED BITS to make their journey as a bird builds a nest. Random things: one bobbin and two needles; a pot big enough to boil a potato; an extra pair of pants for her brother; an extra up-buster for herself. She made a rucksack of a quilt and packed their take-ables within and bound the bundle in twine; Carnival could carry it, that and his ax. She tidied the house daily; she was always good that way. She made a pantomime of her heck box and her corner chair and a stack of waiting mendables like a cardsharp's bluff in case any uninvited should come and think them only out for a stroll but due back soon. Carnival had chopping commitments that kept him in splitting form, and they'd agreed that he'd rely on her to determine when they went. She did her chores—the chickens, the cow—she said her how-dos as she had to, flustered her apron over her growing swell whenever an onlooker double-took, and generally pretended that the future was a long way off.

Inside, she wanted to tell True all. Her friend might advise her, guide her, help her, stop her. She was scared and needed firm direction from someone not the source of her confusion, but Carnival convinced her that he would chop the world to give her life firm footing, yet he could only do that if they kept their slip secret. She had trusted her brother, once, and that was all it took; now to trust him again took all she had. The only thing to escape her lips was her buckteeth, and even those she tried to keep contained lest the sight of them should cause her brother to lick his lips anew. Not a word, she promised Carnival, she wouldn't say a thing. She folded her long fingers over her growing swell and assured him that True would never hear of it from her.

IS IT TIME TO GO YET? Carnival would ask her as he dropped his mendables before his sister each night. *Not yet*, Jubilee would tell him, as she looked anywhere but where all her troubles lay. *Soon*, she'd tell him. *Not yet, but soon*, she'd say. The kind of soon that doesn't come along every day.

ONE WEEK AND AN APRON STRETCH later True came to call with spring rhubarb and a reminder. The Ladies' Tumbling Club would have its anniversary tumble on the Tuesday to come, and Jubilee most certainly would have to be there, she'd missed the past month and, come to think of it, why had she? *I've been busy*, she told True, and True's eyes surveyed busy the way a cat waits out a mouse. *Doing what?* True wanted to know. But Jubilee only flustered her apron and answered with a *this 'n' that*. True took in the swell, the sewing set-up; there was a bundle on the floor by the door that wasn't at all Jubilee tidy. *We'll walk there together*, True decided, *and have us a nice long talk about this 'n' that on the way.* Jubilee—what could she do on the spot? She nodded okay.

A-TUMBLING SHE WOULD GO.

The swell was gaining weight daily and she could feel the drag of it in her shoulders and her back, as if her other body parts were being pulled into the eddy that was aswirl in her guts. Pulling, too, was her high bust, less high by the day, weighing down her up-buster and more drupaceous than any juicy succulent that might dangle heavy and drop. Only her legs were spared the draining maelstrom that afflicted most of her upper half; though they, too, shared in the full body effort to make Jubilee miserable by puffing to Roo Drell proportions—knock-knees to knock-ankles, hock solid. Lifting them to walk felt like walking underwater, and walking underwater felt to her the new improbable miracle.

Carnival was unelated by his sister's determination to take one last tumble. He was proud of that swell, proud and scared of it, afraid to want it but afraid of losing it, too. He said to his sister no, but it wasn't much of a bark, and she said more than words back—she took the rucksack by the door and unpacked the bobbin and the needles, the pot, the pants, the up-buster, folded the quilt that made the bundle and returned it to its trunk, then sat splay-legged in her mending chair and dared him to say no again. The stray dog in him knew to keep from scratching at that door until it was she who reopened it without prompting. After the no passed on, she hoisted herself out of her mending chair and repacked the quilt with the bobbin and the needles and the pot and the pants and the up-buster and placed the bundle on the floor by the door once more. She'd tumble, and he'd have no say.

THE DAY CAME to go and True was crack o' dawn punctual. There was a dog in the yard but its teeth were soft as corn kernels and if there was any bite in them it was mash. Not even the ax blade it was honing was menacing enough to panic a bumblebee. When True stepped around it she heard a mute growl, or maybe she only imagined it, and so she did what the cur couldn't, she grit her teeth at it and grrr-ed. The house again was tidy, the pantomime artfully disheveled, the bundle by the door looked a bit different to True but a bundle nonetheless and un-Jubilee all the same. And un-Jubilee all the same was Jubilee herself, who looked to True about as full of *this 'n' that* as any soul who had ever come and gone. As they went to go, there was no need to further chasten the dog in the yard; it was drool-eyed and belly down and had neither bark nor wag. True and Jubilee stared it down as they passed, and once past, Jubilee stared back at it to keep it down, and that was all the no it needed. They were down the road and beyond the blind of the bend when the dog found its bark and took to the woods with its ax.

HEAVY LEGS, HEAVY HEARTS, it was so slow going, going to tumbling. True wanted to talk about *this 'n' that*— how things had come to this, and how this had led to that. Jubilee was swollen, yes, but torn. She'd promised Carnival she wouldn't say a word, yet wanted for all the world to confide her troubles to True before she and her brother ventured off into the great unknown. The silence between them was slow as a slow step, drawn out and waiting, waiting for the next silence, waiting for the next step. You'd think in a small world words would be safe things to take on a walk, to fill the time between where you start and where you'll end. Two close friends passing through trees and knee-high grasses with only bugs to hear them should not feel constrained by any earthly ties to keep from each other the things that need to be said now and then about this 'n' that. Walking, you'd think, through a landscape made what it is by any number of improbable episodes—lightning strikes, magmatic upthrusts, flowers and trees that need bees to be seeded—such odd and natural examples of what goes into making the world spin round would give even the most impacted words on the most profane subjects all the laxative they need to ease out and be free. But Jubilee, true to her word, kept it all in, making the air and the hours between them swell with the bloat of awkwardness. Several times True would be on the verge of a word like jumping off a cliff, only to have Jubilee look downcast and away as if to say she was not ready for such a leap, so True would step back, and they'd walk on, waiting for the next silence, waiting for the next step. It made for slow going, going to tumbling all the slower, and the swollenness between them all the heavier, all the way they walked.

IT WAS QUITE the bumptious spring gathering for an anniversary tumble. Threesie Lope was already high on the rise and throwing her arms in a cartwheel like a tree buckling in a storm. Tucked in a tuck like the tuck she took to at home was Loma Soyle, giving the day a what-the-hell whirl as she, too, rolled down the ridge in a path for her sister to follow; Petie'd feel it with her shoulders and her knees, or so it was hoped. Frainey Swampscott was a sideways stinkbug picking up speed through knee-high pussytoes on her downslope rollaway, and had Knotsy O'ums not been so triple jointed in her flimsy put-together she might not have undulated out of Frainey's way in time to avoid being splattered. Onesie waved hello from a one-armed handspring, and Twosie yelled it as soon as she regained the wind her unsuccessful somersault took away. There was a fluttering fanfare a bit removed from the rest—it was Zebeliah Hackensack, on a hillock higher with a pitch to it south of the rest. She was inexplicably decked out in hip waders and a saddle blanket cinched at the waist with a strop and latched in place with an ice hook, and dangerous as her getup appeared, it was thought best that she tumble a bit farther afield from the others. Should she get hurt, she'd yell, or so that was hoped, too.

True was in full glee. She smacked her hands in a clap you could hear cross-county. *What fun!* she announced to the air and the grasses as she took in the girls in the air and the grasses. A small cluster of audience called out encouragements from the fringe. *Once more unto the breach!* Kennesaw bellowed, and every time he did, a wearied tumbler would regain the hill to start her downfall anew. Hunko offered his huzzahs, mostly cackles and catcalls, and Luddy chimed in with a cattleman's whistle, yet between them their airy adulations did not add up to the solid admiration that Carnival always brought to the proceedings, and for the briefest moment, Jubilee missed her brother's presence, his ax and his devotion, the sweating swell of him beating in the grass like a one-man band.

True checked her coiled bun and repinned it, scalp tight, then swatted Jubilee on her buttocks and didn't even wait for her friend to neither accede nor demur, she stepped a foot in front of a puffed leg and gave Jubilee all the push she'd ever need. As Jubilee tripped forward True got her hands smack on the girl's swollen ankles and lunged herself airborne and beyond, and as Jubilee rolled to avoid crushing her swell, True pulled Jubilee's ankles with her to bring the revolution full circle. Jubilee grabbed True's ankles in an effort to jam the roll, but it only added thrust to their rotation. *True!* Jubilee yelled, but True wouldn't heed her. Again, they went over, and again, and again. *True, stop!* Jubilee yelled, but her voice seemed to have no momentum of its own. There were hollers and whoops coming from rolling clusters across the grasses. There was a *whoops-a-daisy!* from Twosie, whose saults might take till summer to perfect, and the *oof!* that rang out from somewhere was either Petie Soyle wheezing through a cartwheel or Zebeliah Hackensack impaled on her ice hook or Knotsy O'ums oozing. Bodies in motion, round and around. The little white buds off of matted pussytoes were clinging to every head as it circled by like many little moons in a crush of galaxies.

This! True said as she came up from her back and started a new lunge forward, *will take care of that!* she continued, while airborne, to the swell on its back beneath her.

There was an *oh!* there was an *ow!* there was an *uh!* there was a *huh?*

There was a rhythm and a precision and a poetry to pain.

There was a *no!* from below coming higher, growing louder.

There was a flash like a flare from the sun come undone.

Hack and swing, came the flare, flashing closer, swinging wider.

From the *no!* came the howl, came it primal, *Jubilee!*

BODIES THAT HAD SWIRLED in motion stopped, stilled by Carnival's voice as if it were the hand of God and not a sound that had come out of nowhere and crushed them each and every like bugs with a smack. Jubilee was a crumpled bundle on the ground clutching at her swell and huffing with the kind of urgency it takes to keep the last few embers of a fire from snuffing out. There was no blood, no obvious bruising, no femurs poking through her flesh, some sweat, a few splits, and pussytoes galore, but absent those was Jubilee's terror.

True was on her knees by Jubilee's side, holding up her friend's head, holding her trembling hands firm, firm but impenitent, *there, there now*, she said, giving Jubilee's frightened eyes the answer they were desperate for: *that has not happened. This is not that. Not yet.*

Carnival threw down his ax a pussytoe's width from True, and threw himself down on both knees by Jubilee's other side, splitting the seam of his denims as he did. True didn't flinch from the blade so close—she'd been cut worse in life and had no fear of mere flesh wounds. Carnival threw off the hand that cradled his sister's head and replaced it with his own, and before he did the same thing to the one that held his sister's two hands in a single grip, he gave the gripper a shove that could fell a tree. True grabbed for the ground to break her fall before the fall broke her, but all she could grasp in the instant of felling was pussytoes in one hand and the ax blade in the other.

Threesie shrieked, *True!*

Loma screamed, *Beast!*

Kennesaw yelled, *Carnival!*

Jubilee cried, *No!*

Hunko and Luddy went for Carnival like they were wrestling a steer for branding, as he bucked they pulled him away from his sister, away from True, away from a moment in New Eden that had no precedent. To all gathered save three, it was a rescue gone awry; Carnival's heroic arrival in the nick of time came too rushed for reason, or so it was reasoned. He saw his sister down, and True down, too, and of the two his sister was the one his concern was for. He was a hothead where his sister was concerned, everyone knew it, a hothead who burned a little too south for his sister, everyone knew that, too, yet most dared not imagine how hot down south he burned for her, and save for the three of them, him and her and True, the three of them who knew otherwise, the contretemps was but a misunderstanding; it could happen to anyone, and it was hardly reason enough for such a miscarriage of civility between close old friends.

Carnival rid himself of Luddy and Hunko and scooped up his sister in his arms, grabbed his ax and lay it over her in his arms, and with all he ever wanted in this world in his arms, he set off bounding down the hill. With him lumbering and her bouncing and the ax flashing with every jump, it was like watching a big, lit log throw off sparks as it tumbled away from a fire.

13. FRAINEY

YOU'RE COMING HOME with me and that animal can rot to Kingdom come, True told Frainey. There were tears coming out of the pillows of her eyes as she made her voice irrefutable. Frainey had not seen eyes leak emotion since the day her parents went in the ground. She had seen nothing more in those days than Chippewa's emotionless eyes, those cold bone buttons dry as drought staring back at her every time the goat wanted, wanted, wanted. Nor had she heard words. Human. Vocal. Outside of her head. Words damp with intent and concern. True's tears made her words swell in front of Frainey's eyes. If True's words had been gashed into a stone tablet by a stab of lightning they couldn't have sounded any more almighty, and it seemed they penetrated the layers of evolution that Frainey had to claw her way back up from because her eyes flashed with the first human re-action True had seen from her all day. Moisture.

True eyed the house, then Frainey, then reason.

Do what you have to, she said.

Frainey nodded. Her tongue was still hard lodged in her mouth, a catch of sticks and leaves damming a stream, but True could see she was trying to clear a path for words, the first to minnow out in many days. It hurt to watch Frainey's body wrench itself into a speaking state. She gurgled like a pump back-washing with air. She choked out an initial *I*, and swallowed hard, and paused to catch her breath, and with even more strug-gle forced up a dried husk of *will*. It took all hers to do so. She had to cull it from the very ends of her being to bring it out of a cave into the open. True softened towards her a bit—a bit. She guessed the effort to say those five letters—no peon heaving blocks of stone to raise a stepped-up temple probably ever exerted more.

SUCH IS THE WAY life becomes a drama. The story starts with a fever and becomes a double departing, then a hole in the ground makes an orphan and sadness turns it wild. Every story's beginning has its own abandoned ruin buried under the jungle of what came after, and no one can say why one thing or another caused this or that, nor after a while which thing caused what. The ruins under the jungle are many, some big, some small, all telling, but there's no telling for certain what they really tell. So we grab on to something to give blame a foundation that isn't a hidden block of stone; instead, something over which we have the power to point away from ourselves or the random fall of fate and say you, you, you, or in this case, goat, goat, goat.

Frainey didn't make herself a wild thing. Her parents' passing didn't make her a wild thing. Chippewa didn't make her a wild thing. The fever did. But a fever is air, and if you can't see air, how can you avenge it?

Do what you have to do, True told Frainey. Was life in New Eden ever anything other than this?

Frainey was scrubbed clean and naked to the day and closer to human than she had been since when. They were outside looking up at the porch and at the front doorway and at the goat standing in it with its back end facing out, and as they passed that single thought wordlessly between them, the goat simply flicked her tail at them and dunged.

IF TRUE HADN'T BEEN THERE to witness it, if she hadn't seen it and smelled it and heard it and buried it under the jungle of her own ruins and sprinkled about bits of it like little arrowheads, not a one would know Frainey's lifelong bugaboo or about the day she set herself free.

True had told her to do what she needed to do and Frainey knew, she just knew. The hand was a mere step ahead of the head when she went to the barn and plucked the key off the peg on the beam and went to the back stall where her grandfather's trunk with the lock on it sat and clunked that key into the lock and chunk went the cog and the hinges squealed like little pigs but sounds didn't matter anymore—in that locked trunk was a handled blade that would put any sound to sleep. The blade was worn and chipped (it had cut through something that didn't take cutting lightly), and the cutting edge was dark rust with what once must have been old red. The handle took to Frainey's hand like a friend remembering, and the smooth worn wood of it said words to her she had never before heard but understood the meaning of like a grandfather's kiss. There was something else in the trunk with it—two somethings, two small bird nests, honey-colored with age, and resting in one like a forgotten egg was a blood clot of dried-up gristle no bigger than a mushroom of dung, and in the other, the same thing, only much smaller.

You go through one door and the world changes you; you go through another door and you change it back. Frainey came out of the barn a naked warrior, blood-lusted and sword on high, everything about her girded, and, as True later recalled, even her eensie-teensies seemed perked for battle. She passed by True in the yard with eyes fixed on the house and the front doorway and the squirming atrocity within. She didn't look at True, didn't try to cough out any words, she went in the house and shut the door behind her. The deed was on. She was doing what she had to do.

True didn't see what actually happened, she heard it, or turned what she heard into a version of what happened. The scuffle of hoof as it skidded on wet dung and slopped straw across a wood plank floor. Snapping sounds, crackings, chairs maybe, or tables, definitely crockery shattering, lots of it. There were thuds big enough against walls that they must have been bodies, Frainey's or Chippewa's, or both, and the whole house shook with each hard slam, windows rattled and whatever panes hadn't been bashed out now fell out. Then one goat moan. Only one, low and done. Then silence.

June riffed in the leaves and a few bird beaks knocked wood off a ways, but beyond that all was summer peaceful, out and in.

True might have entered the house after a pass but the stench exhaling from it suddenly grew stenchier. Something in the dung pungency and the blast of splattered urine and filth had an added odor, something fresher was in it now, a gush of something intestinal, bloody, vile, a stink born of life coming to an end. True, for one of the few times in her life, was scared now for her friend, truly scared. *Frainey?* she called into the dark stench, *Frainey?* But Frainey didn't answer. True was ready to steel her lungs and stomach and enter. *Frainey?* she called one last time, but Frainey didn't answer again, so True put one foot on the porch step to start her climb to who-knows-what, and before she placed both feet on that mission Frainey's voice met her halfway. She called back out, *Mama? Mama?* It was a shock. The voice. The words. The words were wrong, but at least the sounds came. Right? That's what True's always said. At least the sounds came. There are worse things in this world than being wrongly called Mama.

The front door opened and Frainey emerged into the end of the day, bloodied but not bleeding, bruised but not blackened, smeared but not caked, spent but not broken, numb but not lifeless, moist-eyed but not crying, untamed but not wild, human but not entirely. She had the handled blade in one hand, with so much blood on it and herself that True couldn't tell which one was bleeding. She was clutching a glob of something with her other hand and it too, hand and glob, was blood on blood confused. She passed True, didn't look at her, didn't say another word, didn't even look to True like she had mistakenly called her Mama, didn't even matter anyway, Frainey was headed back to the barn and the

134

stall in the back and the trunk that had been her grandfather's and she would get there like a mist gets where it's going.

True crept after her silent as fog herself and watched Frainey lift the trunk lid and listened to the hinge pigs squeal, and saw her place the bloodied blade back inside the box. And the other thing, too. First she moved the smaller of the two pieces of gristle that looked like dung mushrooms into the nest with the bigger one—now they looked like mother and child gristle sleeping as one. Then into the empty nest she placed the bloodied glob. It was fat and fatty; tubes off it were chop cut and dripping. It didn't look to True like anything she had ever seen, but then it did, and when it did, something in her seized—the same thing that seized in Frainey at the sight of the key. It was a heart. It was Chippewa's heart. It too would shrink to gristle one day resembling something it once was. Frainey shut the lid and looped the lock and clunked it closed and hooked the key on its peg on the beam and what little came of her life from that moment on was hung there, too.

14. MAWZ

MAWZ HAD PICKED SO MANY jack-in-the-pulpits for her it was years before they grew back, and they never did grow back as plentiful. In some spots they never grew back at all. Mawz was the only jack-in-the-pulpit True would ever allow herself in life, and it became a bare spot on her heart. It wilted on the front porch that night and withered at the root and never bloomed again in her for her mother or Mawz, or any other potential mate in town, or any other person at all, really, except maybe Frainey Swampscott, but that was purely from animal instinct. There had been no explanation from Cozy, the night was a tornado with no warning—it hovered high high for the moment to tail and touch down and destroy, and whistled back up into thin air as swiftly as a splinter.

TRUE HAD GOOD CAUSE to pound her Drell fist on her Minton palm, to stomp her Buckett feet and wail a Lope cry, but she did none of that that night or ever. On her face she fastened a smile as taut as barbed wire and from that night on it was the only expression she allowed her mother to see; and for Mawz she didn't even bother to fasten the wire to fenceposts, she'd give him the whole spooled bale. From that night on if she saw Mawz approaching she crossed to the opposite side of the street, she swam on the far shore, she climbed trees in a part of the forest where he never touched bark, and doing so convinced her mother that she was safely out of those woods. Cozy never told her the truth and True never asked to know, and deep in that gulch of unknowing is where mothers and daughters perish.

BULL ENGERSOL'S PASSING WAS a hushed ordeal. It was the following summer on the very day that the annual dance at the Grangery would have fallen, had the annual dance not been canceled, had the last summer's dance not been the last summer dance, the last dance of any dances. It was Mawz who told Luddy Upland that Bull had gone riding out beyond the ridge above Grunts Pond, that he had been startled by a snake by a bear by a snapping limb by a funnel cloud by a gunshot, he wasn't sure, but the horse spooked and the saddle straps snapped and Bull's hitting a rock headfirst spelled doom. Mawz said he took a guess as to where his father had ridden and followed his trail like a good little Indian and found poor Papa on the ground with his brains spilling. Mawz said Bull didn't have his best friend Remedial Bliss there to roll that rock out of the way so his head wouldn't hit it. Mawz said, Luddy said, that Bull had always said he'd meet a no-good end for reasons he'd rather not say, and so he did, and Luddy said Mawz said *'nuff said*.

Bull's passing was a snake a bear a snapping limb a funnel cloud a gunshot, and following it not too many cold winds after was the lowering of Cozy's pine box in the ground to an eternal destination unknown. True slung her barbed-wire smile around the gulch in the ground where the box was placed. Jubilee held her hand and Threesie Lope kicked the first clod of dirt in for her. Kennesaw was there, Hunko, too, Frainey, Zebeliah, Carnival had dug the hole, the Soyle sisters stood around it with Onesie and Twosie, Knotsy felt faint and collapsed into the arms of Elementary Hurlbutt, he was still vertical then, or was it Luddy Upland, one of them in any case, they kept an eye peeled for any movement behind any distant tree, the quickest swish of a horse tail that might be Mawz, but as far as they knew he never showed.

HOW TWO PEOPLE COULD keep their distance in a small town is a big mystery with few clues to follow. True never once stood face to face with Mawz again from the day he asked her to a dance to the day he took his last step, it was thirty years or more, that's a lot of trees to hide behind. True's youth crested in fewer years than it takes an apple sapling to bear its first fruit, and the skin around her eyes and mouth was as tight as her resolve to make a life for herself free of pink velvet ribbons and foot warmings and foolish dreams. She threw off her girlhood like a pair of dancing slippers and took up the thick woolen socks of practical contentment, tending her own garden, seeding her own rows, and partaking of social interaction only when there was the remotest hope of delivering a good tongue lashing.

It was in those years of growing old fast and growing cold faster that True started her tradition of serving tea to Kennesaw Belvedere on his birthday, of admonishing Jubilee Aspetuck to stay a minimum of two family portraits away from her brother lest they become the picture of ruin, of giving Hunko Minton what-for

for whatever reason on a daily basis, and of staying one suspicion ahead of Threesie Lope at all times.

It was this latter endeavor that consumed True and made her braid grow gray with care. Onesie Lope was a jumpy girl who flinched at the slightest belch or hiccup. And Twosie was endurable company until she opened her mouth and last week's mutton got re-served. Threesie, however, was as close to True in temperament and steely coolness as if she had herself been on the blown-out end of a punctured romance and had grown tired of the whole game of mating. To True's knowledge there had been no boy in town sniffing at the hem of any one of the three Lopes. They were in fact known among the boys as hear no evil, speak no evil, and pure evil, though no one dared utter this to them directly.

Threesie was the one of the trio who could go too far with a look, a prank, a complaint and not stop until she had covered more ground than a winter howler, and this charming attribute was what many considered to be the reason than not even a distant cousin wanted to sled down her hills. True admired this. She had, in a way, become like her own mother, taking comfort in Threesie's disdain for the other half of the human equation. But True wasn't entirely cozy playing Cozy; she knew too much about her own heart to trust that Threesie had come upon her abjuration of all things male in an un-prodded manner. Some boy at some time somehow pulled some stunt that sent Threesie reeling, and True would wonder all her life who the wounder was.

Threesie claimed she came upon her spinsterhood as one would a case of childhood mumps, a random contagion settled upon her with a fever and a rash and an incurable aversion to warm feet. Twosie insisted that Threesie had never been sick a day in her life, and as sure as the Lopes had tripe last Tuesday, as evidenced by what accompanied Twosie's testimony, Threesie had, at the age of ten, convinced Mawz Engersol to pledge their friendship in a bond of saliva, and having done so, she was convinced that once their spit had spun together, he would never drool over any other girl in town again.

To Threesie's dismay, Mawz was already dry in the mouth when it came to True Bliss. When True watched him horsing in the fields, his tongue felt stiff and heavy; when the girls went tumbling and he was watching her, there was an unexplainable bubbling in his innards, and afterwards he'd have to excuse himself and dive into Grunts Pond to cool down.

Threesie didn't make Mawz's juices flow. Not one of the Lope triplets had that ability. Ask Frainey Swampscott, who knew a thing or two about the strange attractability of animals, and she'd opine that it was because the Lopes were born in a litter, and anyone born in a litter had little chance of becoming anything other than a pet. Frainey used to say that it wasn't a surprise that the Lopes shared more with the animal kingdom than the righteous one, after all, their mother, Whinnie, looked like a horse, and their father, Boyle, acted like its ass. It was hard to argue with such logic, at least as far as Whinnie Lope was concerned, for she had thick fetlocks like a mare and a face made for a feed bag, and although none had ever observed her in her birthday suit, it was not an unreasonable hunch that the mane trailing down her neck gave purchase to a tail. Whinnie Lope was also tall. Inhumanly tall. Taller in fact than the horse that threw Bull Engersol, seventeen hands tall at least and a few extra fingers thrown in. Frainey went so far as to surmise that Bull Engersol's horse may have indeed been Whinnie Lope's father, and there was no denying she had its eyes and hooves.

Unfortunately, no one ever got around to proving this, and any hope of doing so ended with Bull Engersol. By the time Mawz found his father's mount wandering riderless in a field of buttercups and black-eyed Susans, he wasn't concerned with asking for or notifying the stallion's next of kin, he was more eager to bury it on top of True's true father, so whatever Whinnie's equine link may have been remains as much of a guess as Bull's spook. As to Boyle Lope, what can you say about a horse's ass, except that you always have to clean up after it. Pure manure, Zebeliah would say to Frainey about her theory, but it was hard to refute the fact that the only buzz of excitement the Lope triplets ever attracted was from flies.

A PERSON CANNOT UNDO the turnings of time anymore than a rock can throw itself. True Bliss took to wearing her braid as a lariat roping her head, grayer as the years advanced, tighter as each new season for jack-in-the-pulpits bloomed and spent. The Lope girls came to accept their unloveliness as a tree split by lightning finds the wherewithal to go on, and as long as the sap flowed through their veins they could endure the scars and gnarls that erupted on their limbs.

Even after True had given Threesie the pink velvet ribbon from the night she never went to a dance, and Threesie promised to always cherish it, to never lose it, to never give it away, only to claim so many years later that she misplaced it who-knows-where, True never would be certain that her friend was really her friend. All of life was puss in the corner to Threesie Lope, a fake-out that got another mouse trapped, and True suspected that as far as Threesie was concerned, maybe Frainey had a point about the Lopes and their animal heritage, and that deep down in the cesspool of the Lope family genes, all cute little mice were really rats.

Threesie was slippery with another feint, too, a fooling, a fakeout behind True's back. She was careful to

keep secret that once a year she helped Mawz Engersol
keep a mourner's ritual, out on the ridge above Grunts
Pond where he had built a mound of boulders over the
tomb of Bull and horse. Once a year on the anniversary
of his father's spooking, Mawz would roll another stone
over the hole to force the bones down lower. Threesie
hoped to win him over at last; she helped him pick jack-
in-the-pulpits to lay upon the rocks to rot, and following his lead, she dug down deep in the pit of her feelings for him and ushered onto the spot her spit to join
his. In thirty years of silent service, she hoped Mawz
would finally say to her the words she longed to hear
from him, but he never did say boo. Instead she only
heard him utter one sentiment ever, and he'd say it every year, over and over, to the bones beneath the stones:
*if only it wasn't true . . . if only it wasn't True . . . if only it
wasn't: True.* Threesie didn't need a prospector's map to
understand the lode buried in that claim. She had horse
sense enough to accept when she'd been pussed. Mawz
was forever on the threshold of True's front porch with
jack-in-the-pulpits in a mound to take her in his arms to
a dance. He was never more than a stone's throw from
that night all those summers ago. And no one had been
more careful in all the years since to keep True away
from the man who broke her heart than this man who
broke her heart. Such a hard rock was his fidelity to
True that it finally beat Threesie's heart into something

approaching human. And so to Mawz she gave a sign, not in words, not with spit, nor with claws drawn or manure piled high, that the girl his grief was tied to was still as tied to him.

IT WAS A SNAKE a bear a snapping limb a funnel cloud a gunshot that lay to rest the spook that haunted Mawz Engersol. Buzzards had come early to snack on him in the small hours of his annual pilgrimage thirty years to the day, and Threesie didn't feel right leaving her armfuls of jack-in-the-pulpits on top of him where the birds would only scarp away the blooms to peck at his guts. She carried the mound down the ridge and across two fields and laid them on True's front porch as gently as she might a baby, she rummaged a scrap of brown paper from the burn can in the yard and with soot on her finger wrote the letters M and E and tucked the note under the neck of a pink bloom.

By that evening, fatigue would wear down True's gall to a nub and air the raw wound at the root of all those rotten blooms. In the morning had she known it was Threesie she would have marched across two fields and given her friend a piece of her mind and a slap. But by nightfall, her tongue had lost its urges and her palm was too busy as an eye sop to swing itself. It was days and days before Luddy Upland found the desiccated bits on the rocks on the mound on the ridge, and he told Kennesaw to tell Carnival to tell Jubilee to tell Threesie to tell True.

What he kept to himself was a slender bit of business that only a ghoul would find comforting. There was a hand there; it had fallen between two rocks, out of reach of pecking beaks, where maggots weren't turning it white it was going black. Luddy poked it from its crib and saw a clot in its craw, a flash of color that wasn't blood. The stiff blackened fingers held something soft in a grip that wouldn't let go. It was a pink velvet ribbon. Luddy thought of prying it loose, thought of burying it, thought of leaving it alone. In the end, he let nature make the decision. He'd found the hand there with the ribbon in it, so maybe that was the way it was meant to be. Mawz Engersol spent his life just out of reach of that ribbon, stopping himself from grabbing it, and once he'd had it, he'd had it. Luddy figured Mawz would have left an entirely different impression on folks if only it wasn't true.

15. Rutherford, Rufus, Roo, and Ruff

THE SUN WAS HOT in its slate blue sky and in no hurry to get itself anywhere. Rufus Drell was the one who said to his father and his son as they neared the lone oak and its wide brim of leaves: *let's stop here before we go on.* Rutherford Drell was a man who remembered hot days, always had a hotter one to compare the present one to, never missed a chance to assure that comparing, but even he'd have been hard pressed to recall a day hotter; maybe not. He'd walked this field many a hot day, cold too, and was around as a boy when this field was teeming with trees. Oaks mostly. His old skin wore every hot day since then. His bald head and thick neck, summer and winter, were permanently aglow as a roasting chestnut. Rufus had sense enough to wear hats, but he wasn't one to wear sleeves, so he had arms the color of his Pop's top and a neck like a bathtub ring. And then there was his boy, Roo, thick in the head and thicker in the calf. Wore a hat, wore a neck rag even, had arms that cottoned to a sleeve, but couldn't fit a full trouser down his legs for all the denim in dandyville. Had to cut half the slack to above the knee, shorts high, for only a thigh's width could make it over the boy's shin hocks. And those hocks like his Pop's arms and neck and his Pop-Up's top were colored you-guessed-it. Roo's dog, Ruff, fit right in with those three—wheat stalk limbs and a trunk the color of bark, which, incidentally, he couldn't. If you put the pieces of all four together, they made up one dark man from deepest elsewhere.

Where they were headed is like asking a nomad for directions. They were a family who had it in their blood to walk and walk, in circles mostly. Wanderlust is usually a fine trait in a farmer. Yoke him to a plow and set him bent on adventure and acres will line up for the kind of back and forth he's crack at. Drells had the back and forth down, had the roundabout, were cartographic when it came to the hither and home, but yoke them to an actual purpose and they could not track. Rutherford Drell was the last of the three to physically have a yoke strap bound round him and a cut blade between him and a steaming team, but that was so long ago the sun was a teenager. He'd taken it up the one time, day after his Pop's box was dropped, and before the sun dropped he dropped that plow and never did a drop of work from whence on. He'd have a life pinned on aimless, and he'd pass it on to his son who'd pass it on to his son whose dog didn't need the lesson, he was born fetch-less.

As the sun came of age, Drell farm was left to become unfecund. Tangle berries and broom straw grew wild where corn should have stalked like pickets. Violet-vine had full run of the underbrush and took a stranglehold of anything that needed air. What was wheat back whence the winds suffused with sucker willows, and all manner of thistle and needle and prickler, until every bit of well-tended earth was taken captive by vagabond greenery as aimless in its back and forth, in its roundabout, in its hither and home as the creepers, who let it all live.

NOT A DAY FACED the Drells when they didn't turn their backs on the farm. A phalarope sputtering to them from a marshy bog was all the birdcall they needed to commence a day's hunt for nothing. Rutherford hatless, Rufus sleeveless, Roo half pantless and Ruff hardly dog, they'd wander yonder and beyond with no more reason than that first curious cave dweller from deepest elsewhere had the first time he set off furry to the bone searching for the shriek he heard in the dark. The sound maker wasn't dweller's goal any more than it was the Drells'. It was mere flint for wanderlust to strike against—as good a directive as any to get a man going to wherever it is he currently isn't.

And wherever they weren't is where the Drells went daily. In ambling forays through fields and wood, one day a valley, a dell the next. They'd walk a day west of where they trod a day before because the slightest shift in longitude gave them an altogether different take on their surroundings. Trek after trek after so many years they'd circumnavigated every square acre of New Eden and New Eden only, not a step beyond for beyond be dragons. And once they'd covered all the ground, they'd set off to cover it again. They were aware of a world beyond the invisible border to the who-even-remembers-how-many square miles of the only world they wanted to know, but why did they need to explore any world beyond theirs when not a solitary square acre of theirs ever stayed exactly the same year after year, so never twice was a scene seen the same way. Season after season after so many years the landscape itself gave space to the inevitabilities of life's deciduous cycle—birth and its opposite—happening over and over, sprout retiring to husk, husk making the bed for sprout. Cousins and cousins of cousins altered, too, the townscape in incremental ways as they clear-cut and cultivated and carved their acreage to suit the needs of their day. Change— by nature or by hand—was forever turning the familiar into someplace the Drells weren't on a daily basis, and as long as that unknown called to them, they'd come to it. It was all they needed.

They'd accident upon discoveries. There'd be bones to find, ancient ones, unearthed by a fresh rivulet—pelvis, femur, jaw with tooth. Fresh bones also, of a diurnal wanderer from only a night or so ago, meat still on the rib, eye open. They'd pause and wonder for what refreshment did these carcasses pause in their sallies that made them vulnerable to an instantaneous end? What ordinary impulse were they following? Were they taking in? Were they leaking out? Did they hear the hiss? See the flash? Gather in a split second's recognition that after this, that's that? Roo would nudge the finds with his boot toe, separate an eye from a dry socket, unburden a scapula, but the collective curiosity would end there. Not even Ruff had much interest in sniffing out further details; smell was not one of his four senses. Together, they'd put an end to any wasted intrigue because after this find would be another, and another, and one more after the next after that and there are only so many answers one can hold in one's head. All four would snort their version of *well, I'll be* while they'd already be on their way to wherever it was that they'd next find whatever it was they wouldn't be interested in. Absolutes were not where they were headed.

Wandering is as much rootedness as aimlessness is ambition. Had the screech in the night not drawn dweller out of his dark cave, nor hunger, nor a tingle in his loins that pointed the way to something he couldn't quite put his opposable thumb on, he'd have grown restless on his haunches no matter what and been out of that rock hole just because *out* was not *in*. It's the need for a single moment to shift in shape if only slightly from *now* to *then*, *here* to *there*, *this* to *that*—the unknowable *that*—the gloriously unknowable *that*—that compels the every twitch, blink, sniff, step, and reach. *There* is a world so foreign to *here* it may as well have started from its own celestial scratch back when *that* was a concept *this* hadn't even considered. Following such a course, a single footfall, a breath, a turn of one's head, the feel of invisible wet or sharp on the underside of what your eye can see is all the motion necessary to satisfy the most basic want of *then* to be a different experience than *now*.

Different, yet not entirely unrecognizable. There is comfort in discovering what we already know by heart. The Drells were upright walking proof that the same ground covered trek after trek can be as stimulating to the trekker the thousandth time as it was the tenth, if only infinitesimally altered the tenth time from how it was the first. Dweller went in search of the screech and found rock, tree, water, dune, mountain, desert, tuber, berg, and beast. He felt rain on his hairy head and snow on his hairy feet. The sun seared the pink tip of his hairy spear and drought parched dry as hair his inarticulate throat. He found all these things as he followed the screech from the night, and with every new screech he followed, he'd find the new in the familiar, a new rock, tree, water, dune, mountain, desert, tuber, berg ,and beast. Different though every new thing may have been in proportion, in contour or color from the version he already discovered, it was a relief to dweller that the rock over *there,* while sparkly with mica and not at all hairlessly smooth like the rock over *here,* was nonetheless rock, different but the same. It was like New Eden: a Drell may have been a Drell over *here* but it was a Lope over *there,* and the Drell *beyond* that Lope was a *Minton, different* but the *same.*

The only real difference between dweller and Drells was that dweller had no plat map or marker stakes to let him know the defining limits of his world. It was accidental that he sparked fire with two rocks and bog rot, but with no notion of home he was as mindlessly aimless as the flames he inadvertently created. He heard the screech in the distance, he emerged his dank and hairy self from the cave into the prehistoric morning, and off he went into sulfurous air that no one else before him had ever breathed. He walked and he walked across sands and over mountains, tasted the ice-fresh waters that flowed earth's blood to its many parts, cut his hairy soles on savanna reeds and volcano rock, witnessed a boulder roll from its perch and crush to pulp the skull of a beast below and the next beast he met he brought down his own rock upon to mimic the crush. He walked and he walked across lands of brilliant greens and snows so white and obliterating that his furry self became nothing but a single hair lost in the unfathomable sameness. He ate, he defecated, often at the same time, he found an outlet for his loin tingle and she tagged along. He found an additional outlet for his loin tingle and he too tagged along, and soon both outlets began to weary him with their unfathomable sameness. One day his inarticulateness raised a war cry, first with the mates, later with all they met, he chipped out a bowl, he dipped a finger in his own excretion and drew an arrow on the side of a cliff, he scraped a pelt and draped himself in it, with a honed stone he punctuated all his aimless discoveries with a question mark etched in a fossil and never gave a thought that all of this could end.

Every day that he trekked, he crossed paths with more and more dwellers just like himself. Loin tingle will do that: fill up the world with more of the same. Aimlessness became a worry to him. He was a dweller among many dwellers now in one large expanse. One dweller among so many he could no longer smell his own smell. He began to miss the solitariness of the lone cave, the safety of contained flames, the quiet refuge from the screech in the night. He devised a subdivision and defined within the large expanse a smaller expanse all his own. And when that grew too crowded for his likes he mounded a bouldered berm around an expanse even smaller. And then a perimeter around lands less ample than that. And when he felt himself too much the same as all the other dwellers, he then parceled for himself a tract within a tract within a tract. And there he built his rock walls, and his white pickets, and marked for his own all the world he'd ever want, New Eden. Such comfort he took from this side-by-side solitude. His plat, his little place, with neighbors all around but not within. He hoped white pickets were enough to keep the next door black-eyes at bay, the clanging empty jack jugs, the dark deeds at the back of the corn crib. But white pickets are only good for keeping chickens out of the corn. Out in the wide, wandering open, vastness gave definition to the expanse between *here* and *way over there,* and it insulated Rutherford Drell and his brood from the black-eyes and clanging empty jack jugs and dark deeds that made miseries for their fellow townsfolk, their town of cousins. As long as no other humans and the human frailties that beset them happened upon these three men and their dog, these three men and their dog could go rest their sun-splotched bodies beneath the yawing expanse of the lone oak and believe in their unhurried hearts that they could rest like this, untroubled and unmolested by fellow humans, forever. But heaven had other plans.

16. KENNESAW

INTERVALS OF REST—on a rock, on a stump, and farther on, past where the woods thin and end and give way to a brief clearing of broom straw, against the moss-bound trunk end of a broken lone tree that hasn't seen green for years. It's all that's left of the tree that felled the Drells. So the story goes, that tree outlived the forest it was seeded from until the afternoon so many years ago when heat lightning ended its sesquicentenniary life. So the story goes, a hiss across the sun aimed for a moving target and missed, and brought down this tree with the biggest boot of all. Every limb cracked off as it flattened to the ground, and so the story goes, flattening to a splatter beneath it the four generations of Drells. Four Drells felled in the middle of nowhere on a high summer day by a string of lightning hitting the only tree standing that they were napping under for shade, or so the story goes. Flummox Belvedere swore on the Good Book he saw it happen, but no one saw him see it, so no one knows for certain. Leave it to a hunch—that's history. What is known is that so shaken was he by the randomness of the hand that hissed the sky, a punishment that seemed to follow no crime, that Flummox from that day on was never seen without his neck craned to heaven, always on the lookout for the next spontaneous act of judgment. The broken limbs from the tree that felled the Drells dried out first. Within the year, Flummox hung himself out to dry, too. Kennesaw's old man came to know what happens when you take off a belt and fasten it around your neck and nail it to a beam in the barn and kick out from under you the only thing that keeps you from knowing what will happen. It was Kennesaw who found him; and he kept that belt, that strip of an unjust god that showed some mercy at last, kept it so he'd always remember.

THE HOLE THAT FLUMMOX'S BOX was dropped into was as close to hell as a hole could be dug. Hunko dragged a sledge out to the tree that did the felling and gathered all the limbs he could carry to begin building Kennesaw's heavenly gates.

THAT IT SHOULD ALSO give Hunko something to hang his heart on was nothing Kennesaw knew of or needed to know; it was True who tipped him off to what Hunko was up to, though at the time it made no difference. Kennesaw all but forgot about the "gift" Hunko was hunkering over in his barn like a workshop elf, or so he said. He didn't expect anything *from* Hunko nor *of* Hunko, and so he was neither displeased nor disappointed when the nothing he didn't care about didn't come.

We can't all be kings, Kennesaw thought then. Not every man is special enough to prove himself special in the simplest acts. Some plant a seed and nothing grows; some measure a plank for sawing, measure it twice, and still saw wrong. There must be that kind among us, the ordinary failures, so that those of us who score the ordinary successes—plant a seed that grows, saw a plank that fits—are extraordinary by comparison. It was like that with Kennesaw and Hunko, his short shadow, years his junior and the mismatched son he might have had, had there been a few more years between them and had he and True given the Bliss-Belvedere drum one last good thump at a very early age. Hunko made those gates for him; it took him years to get them just

159

right. How could Kennesaw have closed his heart to something like that? Special, and not special enough. Between them exists something so special no ordinary lockbox has ever been able to keep it locked from his memory for any significant length of time, and he can feel Hunko gaining on him by the second, as if the boy were following him to True's.

Call it a sign or that sock in the eye you don't bounce back from, but what happened that day with the felling of the Drells and the effect it had on Flummox adult-ed Kennesaw from his father's son to his own man in a matter of hours, and put him on the path to the rest of his years with only one real regret trailing behind him.

17. RUFF

A FLEA BITES A DOG; a dog bites an itch—whose story is it?

Let's say it's the dog's, and let's say the dog is Ruff Drell. Ruff's been lounging in a bed of forget-me-nots one sunny afternoon a year or so before his entire family is felled. He's licked every drop of sweat off of his big dogly sac and he's moved on to sampling to his tongue's content the crusty delights that cling to his hind-end outpost. Mid-snack, a sensation takes hold of him that's as annoying in its suddenness as it is in its itchiness. To his consternation, one side of his big dogly sac is penetratingly beset by what feels like the teeth of a shark, digging in and not letting go. Ruff bares his teeth at the interloper and chomps down as hard as he can on that side of his doghood and gnaws away with the hunger of a lost mountaineer at whatever it is that's biting him bald. In his frenzy to dislodge the microscopically flat freeloader with the microscopically ferocious fangs, you might say Ruff responds a bit too roughly. A tidal wave of red fluid is loosed from his big dogly sac that gushes with the urgency of a hungry mountaineer's bowels after dining on his own dog cold and uncooked, and as the fluid flows out, so too does one half of one half of Ruff's big dogly sac, leaving an oozing and rapidly wrinkling half sac that's not a pretty picture. Had the dog any bark in him, they'd have heard it in heaven.

The image sticks because of that flea. Had the flea not bitten, Ruff wouldn't have chomped; and had Ruff not chomped, Roo wouldn't have chopped the remnants of the half of the half that wasn't chomped, and had Roo not chopped the half of the half not chomped he might have gotten around to chopping both halves fully and leaving Ruff with no sac to attack and no self-dismemberment to remember.

Memories hitch themselves to the advancing years howsoever they can. A flea bites a dog and a dog bites itself and a man butchers a job and a small bit of business grows into legend. Which memories come along for the ride and which ones flee the first chance they gel has no formula to regulate their participation in the scheme of things. Add water and sun to ground and seed and a small green sprig of certainty will grow. But *this* added to *that* followed by *then* does not necessarily guarantee that the true story of *whatever* is the memory that's remembered now. Ruff Drell is remembered for two things: for being a dog with one half of his doghood sacrificed by a master who hadn't the heart to do the job fully; and for being a felled Drell. All who knew that Ruff had maimed himself first had kept that bit of business to themselves, and it fell out of common knowledge when all who knew about it were felled themselves. Ruff knew, not Roo, that he had maimed himself not because he was self-abusing, but because a microscopically small intruder with the appetite of a lost mountaineer had hitched a ride on his sac, and if there was anything Ruff could not tolerate, it was a Ruff rider. So he did what any dog would do to put that lost mountaineer out of his misery, only to create a bit too much misery for himself. Ruff went to where all dog bones get buried with a truism buried alongside him, which was that the legend about his lost doghood was a falsehood.

Now take the flea. It hopped from woody mouse to savory chicken to sweaty dog sac, and on that hot and humid ride found itself a feast worth digging its chops into. The flea was only doing what fleas do as Ruff was only doing what dogs and Drells do. Dogs and Drells pay inordinate amounts of attention to their sacs, and fleas bite. The flea had emerged from its larval beginnings as unformed as the day after tomorrow, with both direction and intent subordinate to instinct. It had to have food, that food had to be blood, and beyond that basic necessity, the where and the how and the when of its feeding were as unpredictable in their variables as were the consequences of it getting what it wanted. You could say that all of life in New Eden is like that. You wake up to a day with no absolutes that have to be observed beyond following your instincts for nourishment and excretion and, if you've the interest, industry; and if you've the outlet—that other business. Where the day takes you is the consequence of how you go about following your instincts—the what you choose to eat, the where you decide to excrete, the how of your industry, the who of that other business—and consequent to all those instincts turned choices come the days after tomorrow and the further choices necessary because of those prior choices made.

A boy goes to take a girl to a dance, gets rebuffed by her mother, takes it out on his father, hides away from his village, and ends his days as a maggots' feast; and the friend who knew him best keeps the truth locked deep in his heart and whiles away his own life with someone else's sadness. And whenever one encounters the friend who knew him best, one cannot help but hum the sad hymn that's sung of the love-lost boy who became one with the everlasting air of the world he left behind. And too, a flea, descendant of the one that roughed up Ruff—to be bitten by one now is to hearken back to that barkless dog as he chomped his sac to stop an itch without a thought of what kind of future might befall him.

18: Petie and Loma

Loma Soyle could stretch forty winks into a voyage round the horizon. When she went down, she was down as far as that golden metropolis that sank into the who-knows-where way back in that ancient time when mere mortals would believe any fantastical story you told them. Good thing bed linens aren't the briny deep 'cause Loma wouldn't bubble a breath for long, long as she went under.

Hephelonius Soyle tried her best to rouse her eldest daughter from her slumber loving. Her two girls, Loma and her sister Petie, shared a room off the kitchen under the shadow of an overgrown elm, and the room had just enough room between the two thin beds for a pantaloon to walk between unmolested, so Hephelonius would starch extra crisp Petie's undergarments with the cherry appliqué and the lace trim so that when the pretty things moved, their crisp folds would scratch and crinkle like pinecones going up in flames, and her sister would wake and be so undone she'd near go up with them. That was one solution.

Another solution was to set aside a day of the week when Petie would get her hair washed with oil of camphor in a tub drug to the head of Loma's bed. Hephelonius would pour pitcher after pitcher of warm pure water over Petie's golden curls and the water that didn't turn them lustrous dark with damp fell into the tub with a tinny drum-drum. She'd drop the tin pitcher on the floor by the tub at the head of Loma's bed and commence to massage Petie's golden curls with the oil of camphor, rubbing it into the scalp in slurpy sounding swirls and swoops, bubbling up quite the froth and giving moths for miles fair warning. Petie loved the smell of oil of camphor. She'd have had her hair washed daily if she could, just to live in that biting aroma. Hephelonius was partial to that smell, too, and grateful that at least her younger daughter was born with the same wise appreciation for things you didn't need eyes to enjoy. Loma, if she had to choose between the smell of oil of camphor or having all of her hairs pulled out one by one, she'd yank herself bald. Loma and oil of camphor did not mix.

Loma began her journey as a baby who cried a lot, and grew into a young woman who slept a lot, and if you asked her why she was so selfish to sleep so much while her younger sister was left to have to brush her own hair, clear her own dishes, empty her own slop and deflect the many compliments on how buttercup-pretty she was in comparison to ring-eyed Loma, Loma would fix a stare on you that you just had to slap her out of.

Petie was in possession of many fine qualities that Loma lacked: her head sat directly above her torso thanks to a last-minute change in the direction that her spine curved; her wheeze was not a distraction; and any knowledge of a discomfiting nature would not spend much time in the inner sanctum of her mind. In short, she had a near-quiet, near-empty head, center-most on her shoulders, and milky eyes.

Naturally, as these qualities were Upland qualities from the O'ums side of things, passed on from Hephelonius and her family to her second child, Hephelonius could be forgiven for lavishing upon the daughter who was not her spitting image the bulk of her spit. Loma inherited what she inherited from the Minton end of the Soyle side of things, and the Minton end of the Soyle side of things were not any side of things Hephelonius ever made reference to without spitting, so to mention Mintons was to spit, to talk of Loma was to spit, to talk to Loma was to spit, and, with so much spit generated on her behalf, Loma did what she could do on a daily basis to goad her mother into spit fits that might one day fill a tub that she could then dunk her sister's half-empty head into, and all the way under, so that the wheezy little thing might bubble her last. That was one solution.

Another solution was for Loma to sleep as long as she could until one day she'd be sleeping forever. Her inclination to the somniferous might, to some, be considered a selfish act, as it did to her mother mostly, and to her sister half the time. They could not understand this girl with the off-center head that was too full of thoughts and not a one of them happy about being Petie's sibling. Her every action was ingratitude on a scale of magnitude that would take a person with a full brain and another half brain added to fully comprehend. To Loma's consternation, between them, Hephelonius and Petie came up two-thirds of a brain short, so having the very people who misunderstood her come to understand her was a likelihood as unlikely to happen as a sunken golden metropolis suddenly coming up for air.

Sleep seemed the only way to live through her life. Down she'd go as soon as she could and out for the count as long as could be. She was tired of brushing her sister's hair, and clearing her sister's dishes, and emptying her sister's slop. She was tired of wishing on stars and dreaming of golden metropoli and waking to oil of camphor and burning pinecones. She was body tired, and heart tired, and tired from being so tired. She felt herself in a hole at the bottom of a chasm too fatigued for anything but sinking deeper. She'd curl into a tuck like she was back in her mother's womb and she'd stay that way for hours and hours and more. She'd stay that way in her bed, if that's where she took to, and she'd take that way to stay any other place, too. Sometimes it was in the cold dark beneath the sagging front porch among the spiders and moles. Other times it was in the woods not too far from the field where the Drells were felled. She'd find a spot like something only in a dream: a place no one else had ever happened upon, a misty hideaway where new moss had tiny fresh blooms, a holy ground not even ants would blaspheme, and as it would be in a dream, the locale was always as quiet and dark as the night before the first day. She'd lay herself down on the cushioned ground and feel the dew-dropped green on her cheek. She'd draw into her tuck with her knees up close to where her bosoms never grew and her arms enfolded about herself as much as her own twisting spine would allow, and she'd hope that sleep would overtake her soon and completely. Until it did, she'd lie there and listen to the feel of the beat of her heart. She'd slow her breath. And still her blood. And in that near lifeless state of waiting for finality she'd think to herself over and over: I will wake to a golden metropolis . . . I will wake to a golden metropolis . . . I will wake to a golden metropolis.

To WAKE WAS to be reminded of what life was not, of her sister's favored position in their mother's graces and her own diminished standing in her mother's spit. How one child, an afterthought at that, could stumble upon such partiality just because of a lucky bend in her back, or a pleasing wheeze, or a proclivity for the intoxicant oil of camphor was a boulder of reason ever at battle with gravity that would always nearly make it to the mountaintop of Loma's comprehension before tumbling down, down, down.

To wake was to also confront an unfortunate truth about the haphazardry of life that ran counter to her feelings of turpitude towards Petie. Petie's lucky back bend and her pleasing wheeze and her overall buttercup prettiness were a sight for every sore eye in town, save two: her own. Her milky eyes, set in her near quiet, near-empty head, had never in her life seen the light of day. Loma's eyes had taken in everything the world has to offer, every shape and form, every shade of day, of night, every color from buttercup to periwinkle. She had vision enough to imagine the golden metropolis in all its ancient splendor, while to her sister, be it standing or submerged, all golden metropoli looked alike. Hephelonius had been insistent since the insufficiency was discerned that Loma be the eyes that Petie lacked—to look for her and look out for her—so that Petie might see the world as God's eye sees it, and Loma, as she did so, might see the world as Petie saw it.

It was expected that Loma would take Petie by the hand and guide her through the years. If there was a climb to make then Loma should be the one to say to her sister *two steps up, that's one, that's two*; if a footfall was imminent in her sister's path she should say to her sister *rocks ahead, step left, now right*; if the woodstove was hot to the touch, she should say to her sister *careful now, that's hot, don't touch*; if left with only each other after their mother's passing, she should say to her sister, *I'll always be here, I will*. A life of lead and follow would be what life would be and Loma should tell herself that *this will be enough, enough*.

Loma began her journey as a baby who cried a lot, and grew into a young woman who slept a lot, and in the dappled light that only she could see between the two she was a daughter who resented a lot and a sister who regretted even more.

This hurts my finger, Loma. What is it?

That's a knife.

My arms and legs and neck and face are all itchy, Loma, what are you rubbing on my body?

It's called poison ivy.
I smell smoke, Loma. Where's it coming from?
Your hair.
Am I as pretty as you are, Loma? Am I? Loma? Are you crying? What do tears look like, Loma?
Tell your sister, Loma. Loma! Wake up, Loma!

WHEN YOU CAN'T SEE a way out, the way out is you. Loma's tongue grew tired speaking to and for Petie's eyes. The more their mother insisted on her sacrifice, the deeper Loma retreated into her own heart, slowing her breath, stilling her blood, and becoming actively inert. It was tranquil there. She was neither resentful there, nor remorseful. She would close her eyes and see the world as she imagined both God and Petie saw it—as a beautiful black void of perfect ever-after-ness. As the years washed forward like the hues in a prism that only she could see, Loma tried to spare her sister the hardened black heart that beat at her daily. As a small girl she had swallowed whole a new potato her mother had yet to quarter for Petie; she choked on it and sputtered and spasmed like a rat on arsenic until she flailed herself against the hot woodstove and miraculously dislodged the spud as if from the ground anew. She reasoned she could do the same with the turmoil of her feelings. She'd swallow them as arsenic down her rat hole of a throat, but stop short of dislodging them by throwing herself on the hot woodstove. That thing burned the hell out of her belly.

She tried, so often through the years she tried just that. At the sun's every shadow around the dial, on the green moss of the forest floor, under the sagging front porch among the spotted spiders and the gray moles, at every stiff swish of her sister's starched pantaloons with their pretty cherry appliqué and lace trim, when spring was all diamonds and summer all circles and autumn all hexagons and winter all flat; as the years put new bends in their spines and spots on their hands, when the box with their mother was lowered into the ground and the rich, dark dirt shoveled back over it like a sprinkling of brown sugar on a cake only worms would enjoy, after every encounter with her own reflection in the parlor looking glass, at every washing with the oil of camphor that Loma in her hard heart had to admit was the silkiest substance she ever saw poured—rather than make Petie more sorry for the golden metropolis she'd never seen nor see, Loma curled into her tuck and tried to will her own sinking, wished for it, cried for it, dreamt of it, prayed, but it never did happen the way she envisioned.

PETIE'S INVISIBLE HANDS WERE full caring for a self she could not see. Best she could on a daily basis she brushed her own invisible hair and cleared her own invisible dishes and emptied her own invisible slop while trying to make herself invisible so Loma could continue to sleep. More often than not she brushed hair that was seldom washed, and cleared away dishes that rarely touched food. More often than that she brushed her own hair with a dish, and emptied her own slop into the kitchen sink, and when one day she cleared her invisible hairbrush into the invisible slop bucket and reasoned she'd have to reach her invisible hand into the invisible reek to retrieve it before Loma woke and got wind and got mad, Petie sat down on the invisible woodstove and burned her invisible behind and cried tears neither one of them would see.

The darkest dark of all is the dark that knows no light. Petie could breathe in the oil of camphor and feel her scalp tingle to its touch, but she could not reason out an analogy to its strong aroma in a bold color or a forceful action, having no reference to what colors and actions looked like. She could feel a face for its abundant nose and absent chin, but she could not conjure an image in her mind to contrast to faces not so New Eden in their appointments, nor was it flattery to call her buttercup-pretty when she had no sense of what a buttercup was. Tell her of a golden metropolis full of colonnades and coliseums and so agleam with perfection that all spines are straight and all heads are full and all eyes are all-seeing, but such a tale of visible splendors is wasted when, to understand a thousand words, a single picture is still needed. Petie was alone in a dark that Loma could never fully grasp. To Loma, dark was merely the absence of light, a time of day, a place where dreams didn't need sun to grow, a hue, a mood, a lampless room, a refuge. It was where she could retreat to and then return from, lead herself into and follow herself out of. Loma had all the words and images for dark except the dark that only God and Petie knew. Petie's dark would take a thousand images to convey and not a one would ever be the last word. One word needed no image, however. To Petie, it was the one word that made all the difference in the dark. It was her word for light. The word was *Loma*.

SIBLING YEARS PASS WITH little things going unnoticed. Petie's head had been migrating over time from center-most on her shoulders to the western end of a right shoulder shrug. It was such a small advance daily that Loma could hardly be blamed for missing the shift as it happened on her watch, but she did miss it, and missed something shiftier, too. Not only was Petie's head inching its way east, her neck was twisting its way Egyptian, with her chin directing her head all the way one way even as her body set its course the opposite. You'd think that seeing that sight day after day would make Loma wake up and take notice, but as it was that she slept for what seemed like years on end, who was going to shake her and wake her just to tell her that something didn't look like it was supposed to look—Petie?

Loma could look away, but she could not hear away, and so it was that when a gurgle was added to Petie's repertoire, Loma at long last deduced that something in her sister was amiss. Petie took on the musicality of a fireplace bellows, with a glottal kind of slurp followed by a nasal sort of wheeze. Whether she slept or lumbered or sat or chatted, she resonated like a hearthside recital at all times, all slurp and wheeze, slurp and wheeze, slurpier sometimes and wheezier others.

Petie did not express disturbance with her new discordance. Slurping was a familiar sound at home from when their mother's spitting was in its high water years—a condition as much a result of bad teeth as it was of a bad humor. As Petie could not equate her torquing neck with choking any more than she could make a connection between their mother's tooth rot and slurp juice, with only a sound to go by, she naturally assumed it was a natural aspect of aspiration and not a forewarning of asphyxiation. Thus, she slurped and she wheezed as she unconcernedly went about brushing her own slop and emptying her own hair. Her curving spine twisted her head further and further, and as it did, it caused the air to her lungs to grow thinner and thinner, which led, over time, to the color of her pretty skin turning from buttercups to bluebells.

ONE DAY THE SUN slants down at just the right angle and something your eye never fell upon before all at once takes you by surprise. You notice that long, thick, diseased branch that hangs perilously close to the rooftop over your bedroom and how the droop of it seems so much more severe now that there's no distance left at all between it and the years and years of decayed leaves and moss and broken limbs that are piled up on your sagging roof and rotting what's left of your shingles. You stagger backwards as best you can and you crane your own twisting neck and your newly awakened attentiveness at what is undoubtedly the cause of all that slurpiness you've been half-hearing in your sleep and you speculate as to the entirety of the disaster that you are sure is impending—the limb breaking off and the soggy roof caving in, and yet another door you must shut on yet another part of your family home made unlivable by the slow degradations of time—and because the mere thought of it is as exhausting as any remedy you might take up—you take to your tuck on the parlor divan—at least the roof over that room is sturdy, for the time being—and as you lie there willing yourself to a standstill you wish and you cry and you dream and you pray that your sister is soundly sleeping in her thin bed in the room you used to share when the roof over it collapses and she goes in one quick final slurp and wheeze in the dark. That's one solution.

Another solution is to cease waiting for your sister's end to fall out of the sky, cease yearning for a hole to be dug in your own honor, cease praying for a sunken golden metropolis to rise from the depths and put to shame the all-too-real world you live in, and instead, wake up: brush your sister's hair and your own, empty her slop and your own, cup your hands around her cheeks and force her twisting neck to turn back just a notch enough to let a bit more air pass through for the little time that's left, and accept that what this life gave you may not have brought you to the golden metropolis, but it made you one in your sister's milky eyes. And when the two of you are found long after your long-awaited stillness has finally come to call, you'll be crushed in your two thin beds in your small room off the collapsed kitchen with your twisted heads twisted towards one another like a pair of crumbled Egyptians, and across the narrow space between you, so narrow a space that you never needed eyes to measure what you had there, you and your sister will be holding each other's hands as you enter that beautiful black void of perfect ever-after-ness that only God and Petie have ever seen.

19. Kennesaw

There are acts that happen upon us, and moments that happen for no reason, and if we are to survive what comes our way to finish our rotations around the sun while feeling the sun for its warmth as well as its scorching, then we who are able must deliver ourselves from the aftermath to where we need to go. It was true with the serpent in the garden and it has been true ever since. The snakebite is not what defines a life; what defines it is how we extract the venom.

Kennesaw knew two truths to be his north stars: he could not endure his father's attentions, nor would he risk tempting Hunko with the same southbound

intentions should his own southbound intentions lead
to lands as unchartered as the heavens. To keep himself from exploring the far reaches of Hunko, Kennesaw
resolved himself to journey in a direction opposite his
young friend, and in so doing, he'd be sure to circumnavigate what his life might be in favor of what he told
himself it ought be. Hiding in the woods wouldn't do,
and merely averting his glances when passing in front
of the New Eden Grangery would do less, or pretending to be espying woodpeckers up high and above
when he happened to be strolling completely innocent-
ly down the path to Grunts Pond would do least of all.
Only one measure was surefire, not that there'd ever
been proof. Nowhere was there to be found in any New
Eden lore that he knew of an instance of time turning
back on itself, of a Bliss or a Minton or a Belvedere leaving New Eden and going back to whence they came.
He grew up on the stories of forebearers coming to this
spot from points far flung and flunger, of compassless
dreamers who missed the footpaths worn by others
before them and who in their inadvertence scaled on
foot and hoof the magmatic tips of a mountain range
beyond the town's highest hill, then descended into the
valley where the water and land and forest formed the
Eden which, having nothing better to do, they claimed
anew. But what no passed-down lore celebrated was
a single soul in all New Eden's swelling generations

since who had ever crossed back—who had retraversed the uncompassed paths and retraced mistaken steps to forge newer lives on other inadvertent grounds; others who came upon Eden only to find it lacking what they weren't even sure they were looking for and finding it lacking, left. But Kennesaw decided to do what no one of lore had done before him with or without plan, example, or thought. He'd leave. He'd be the first. He'd find a new New Eden elsewhere. Free of torment. Free of temptation.

With neither provisions nor belongings satcheled, Kennesaw walked out the front door of the Belvedere home with a determination to outgrow the town that he feared would never outgrow him. His gait as damn well determined as his father's, he walked down the road he walks today, past neighboring farms and fields still tilled, past the rise to Tumblers' Ridge and its tickling grasses, past the path down to Grunts Pond and the rock and the life force that down there beckoned. He slowed at the path a bit in hopes of seeing signs of Hunko, and seeing none, was both relieved and disappointed, and presented with a choice, chose disappointment as a lubricant for resuming his former pace. Past Saflutises' fields he walked, past the Bucketts' barn, the Whiskerhoovens', the O'umses'; he followed the virus's path past Nedewen Field and its ever-increasing markers, past True's and her row of apple trees where one of the dozen had recently succumbed to blight, past Carnival who waved his ax to him as he passed.

This walk was an entirely different walk than any Kennesaw had heretofore embarked on. Different because it was a walk of departure, yes, but also, because Kennesaw had about him a new awareness of his surroundings. Landmarks he had passed so often as to not know they existed (much as he did people at times), now produced in him a sensation that if this were to be the last time he took in such familiar and well-worn sights he would indeed miss them deeply, surprisingly, and as this odd sentimentality took hold of his entirety his gait slowed, and his bluer-than-blues sought out details of the everyday that he had never really considered in his day-to-days. That eight shingles on one row and seven on another were missing from the east wall of the Bucketts' hay barn. That Zebeliah Was-She-a-Hackensack-or-Was-She-a-Whiskerhooven did not look too comely from the back end when bent over and digging in her spring flowerbeds. That the O'umses' only offspring set out for airing on the front porch looked not quite human, and more like candle wax readying to be form-poured. That the path down to Grunts Pond that used to be lined with jack-in-the-pulpits and balsam was now nearly bare.

Small and insignificant can be huge when viewed for the last time, and viewed through a nuisance of tears can produce in a man a stubbornness to get on with things. Flummox be damned, Kennesaw thought, as he rid damp sentimentality from his eyes with the back of his hands. He would leave everyone and everything he knew in the past. In time, Hunko would forget him.

His destination? An education. He would fill his head to overflowing with distractions eastern and western. He would learn great things, important things about important people, by important people, historical people, historic events, places, formulas and computations. He would fill his mind with every manner of distraction ancient, modern, and in-between, and so distracted, his mind would circumnavigate his heart and this would suffice as a life. It was certain that he knew his ABCs and his 1, 2, 3s. He knew a square from a circle, and most assuredly, having known the Lopes, a horse from an ass. But what schooling he had had beyond that had its limits. His was schooling done around the kitchen table from primitive primers missing pages and long out of print—primers a young and not-yet-troubled Porcine had rescued from the burn pile in her childhood when her own mother's actions turned unmotherly. As her own mind went wild as an untilled field, Porcine laid these primers out before her own child like sacred texts from a Hebrew's altar, plopped out before him like raindrops, spoke the words and the letters once and expected her child to repeat them forever, which he did; more proof of his outcastedness, Porcine then feared. And no sooner did she lay the books out than she snatched them back and returned them to hiding, learning dried up for the moment, *That's enough,* she'd say, *now heed your father, he's out in the barn, hey Blue Eyes, he's calling for you.* Where Porcine's mother, Agrippa, got the books was anybody's guess; for all Kennesaw knew, they may have been gifts from the ghosts his mother's mother communed with. But thank those ghosts for they lay a foundation that could be built upon. He could read; he could add; he could ask questions and take in their answers like air. Such learning was a short, steep drop-off to knowledge of any practical application, and although dragons lay beyond their limits, he'd more happily slay them than stay put.

THE DIRT ROAD OUT of town led Kennesaw to a roadway of unfamiliar composition, hard and unrutted, wider, with an urgency to its unfolding: it did not even wind itself up and around the mountain range whose magmatic tips prior feet had climbed to blisters. This roadway did not want to waste a moment; it cut right through them. The trees he passed appeared not so green and tall as the ones he climbed as a boy, the roadside flora not as redolent, no funk of jack-in-the-pulpits, no balsam at all. Dwellings off this road were odd long metal structures on blocks that looked to Kennesaw as if they could be dislodged and heaved like hay bales by any strong wind that happened to blow by, and on the way to their front doors was a landscape so cluttered with adornments that surely large winds had indeed passed through. He could not imagine knowledge contained within a can, let alone conceive of any living soul dwelling in such structures that were not even attached to the ground they sat on; a man must have his feet on the ground to know he exists, and so must a house. Farther on there were homes of larger scale, fortress-like as they dominated smaller environs, attached to the ground by foundations built rock upon rock, but with surroundings devoid of any displays, landscapes clipped as precisely as a close shave, and grasses so immaculate, it was hard to imagine any feet, hooves, or paws ever being tickled by so much as a single blade. Nowhere was there to be seen gates shaped as heavenly harps, nothing fashioned with such care as Kennesaw's gates by Hunko's hands, nothing as forgiving, nothing that said I may look imperious, but I have a heart. Knowledge of any use could not live in so unwelcoming a place.

Beyond here, dwellings gave way to clustered groupings in brick and stone: store fronts whose windows beckoned with offers of *2 for 99¢* and *buy 4 get 1 free*; there were no store front porches for gnawing the daily grist on like the New Eden Grangery, no rockers for

taking a load off, and heaven forbid a man who relieved
his bladder by the side of this route. The air hummed
like bees grouping for a kill, and on the street there were
vehicles of every shape and speed that would finish
the job the bees left undone. At every glance was a new
sensation that Kennesaw had only seconds to process
before another took its place. Multicolored illuminants
that flashed and sizzled, great clouds of acrid smoke
that belched from funnel stacks in the sky and from the
vehicles, too. And the people themselves—a monochromatic herd less green and less tall than the folks of his
familiar world, yet sweeter, he had to admit, though in
a sickeningly odiferous way altogether not to his liking.

THE DEEPER INTO THIS unfamiliar terrain he walked,
the more he tried to assure himself that he would in
time lose the discomfort of being a foreigner in this
foreign land in his crisp overalls and tailored buffalo
plaid, but the monochromatic herd whom he passed
did not even look up from the ground as they passed
him by, their downcast eyes did not once connect
with his own bluer-than-blues. How can one become
one with others so otherly if they refuse to even ac-
knowledge that you're you, Kennesaw wondered. He
crossed a thoroughfare with the herd, he followed a
stampede around a corner, he thinned himself to not

touch shoulders with any passersby lest he catch their downcastedness and lose his ability to see what lay ahead, and it dawned on him as he made it from one end of a street to the other that he'd encountered more people in that hundred feet of walkway than he'd seen in New Eden in the entirety of his lifetime. And not a soul thought him anything special.

He'd left New Eden early morning; he'd reached this odd world late afternoon; perhaps he'd find what he was looking for before the sun went home for the night, though his optimism was not so sure-footed. He cleared his throat and approached anyone who slowed to a stop. *Where can I find an education?* he asked them. Most ignored him as they did the hum in the air. A few looked up from their downcastedness long enough to roll vacant eyes of no coloring at all; they either shook their heads or hunched their shoulders or muttered indecencies as they resumed their trajectories to wherever downcastedness must hurry to. One passerby told him to try the school of hard knocks; another said go to a red door on a street named with a number and ask for an Esther-Ann or an Evie, or if he was truly looking to be educated, ask for a Big Joe. A child no taller than Frainey Swampscott's goat said to him, *Uh, duh, the library,* and showed him the way there by spitting it over her shoulder. Beyond where the girl's saliva landed with a crack was a town square swarmed by a herd, and above their shoulders rose a statue of a soldier, in clothing even more unusual than Kennesaw's, aiming his blunderbuss at a low-slung cement structure as long and squat as a loaf of bread. Nothing about its flat facades and windows too high to see through said to him come hither. In front was a sign hand-carved in rough-hewn cedar that for a moment made him think of Hunko's gates, but the sign and what it said quickly trained his heart on feelings elsewhere. The sign read: Library.

Kennesaw entered through an opaque slab glass door that was heavier than gravity in his hands, and once inside, gasped with all the fury of a last breath at the vision before him. What had been an unremarkable exterior yielded its lack of charms to an interior as resplendent as a pasha's caravan. Books of every size and shape, leather-clad, cloth-wrapped, etched, embossed, and embellished, gold leafs and illuminated frontispieces, periodicals, atlases, cartographs, tables and charts, so many tomes, so many subjects, so much of the world outside of New Eden, more than he ever imagined could exist, and here it all sat waiting for his fingertips to bring its essences alive. Oh, how wondrous this paradise of parchment with its smell of history mixed with possibility. Not another soul shared the space with him. Only diffused light filtering through the high windows, settling on every gleaming surface a hush of promise. This is what existence is when Flummoxless, perhaps even

Hunkoless. Here Kennesaw would find the distraction he was looking for.

Shelves of facts and figures and forgetting. He'd begin at the beginning and he would not stop until he reached the end of all that man knew to learn, and so distracted, his mind would circumnavigate his heart as he hoped it would, and this would suffice as a life. He wasted no time, digging in like it was a mouthwatering Sunday Sit Down. He read about Darwin and the voyage of the Beagle, and Galileo's heavenly wonderings, and was captivated by Ulysses and his perilous twenty-year wandering on the wrong route home. He'd open one book and then another and dine on both as he would a plateful of Sunday delectables. Volumes on Descartes, Plutarch, Epicurus—they nourished him as completely as chervil and lovage and a heaping helping of huckleberry slump. Their pages were silk against his skin, the thoughts moving through his dermis and into his bloodstream with osmotic intensity; he absorbed their ink like air. But no sooner had he settled on the teat than a bell with a velvet clanger rang, a bell that might call Frainey's goat home for a bucket of clover, and as it rung out a melodic cling, clang, clung, the illuminants over his head one by one went dark, and slatted blinds descended over the windows that were too high to see through, and he found himself ushered out of his uninterrupted utopia and thrust abruptly back out the slab glass door, outside the low-slung loaf of bread, a plate cleaned of all treats but the ones he had no taste for—the shops, the acrid smoke, the vehicles, the hum, the herd. The moon was rising. He had not accounted for a time limit to his escape—escape, he was led to believe, is a sail always finding the wind, an adventure in perpetual self-invention, endlessly struggling against odds and ogres, but this escape had soft treacheries: a velvet bell and illuminants gone dark, and a door that locked from sundown to dawn. He had not thoroughly thought through this endeavor, brought no provisions with him, nothing in a satchel for bunking a night under the stars. And then there was the matter of currency, of which he had none. Not an eagle silver to his name, not a Jefferson two dollar (when's the last time anyone in New Eden had traded currency for hospitality?) and without such, he could not buy what he lacked, not a meal and surely not a bed. Not even his bluer-than-blues could do his bidding here among the downcast, of this he was certain, although for a moment he was tempted to seek out Big Joe, but wasn't that kind of curiosity what compelled him to leave Hunko behind and lose himself in a world of facts and distractions? Better not. Inside the library, the entirety of man was his to access for free; but free comes at a cost, and Kennesaw, for all his cleft and chisel, for all his crisp hems and darted buttonholes, for all his superior good looks and bearing was, among the herds on the streets of this odd town, unlike among his own, nothing but a bum with empty pockets, and despite the bounty that could be his at *2 for 99¢,* was too broke to do anything but leave and make the long walk home. With no other choice, he would make every day a twenty-year journey: leave home every dawn and return to his mother's dinner table of boiled rocks every night, to his father's demands, his Scylla and Charybdis, Ulysses of the daylight. Dawn after dawn. So this he would do, and it would have to suffice as a life.

And for many years it did. Marco Polo and Magellan, Charlemagne and Columbus, Socrates and Plato, he followed every tale, every bit of wisdom, to a new piece of knowledge. From first rays to dusk his mind was occupied by a world of thoughts so far from New Eden and the lore that was his provenance that this library and its contents may well have been one of Galileo's celestial orbs in the unchartered regions of the universe and not simply a room full of books in a building in a town on the other side of a hill beyond the end of the gravel road that formed the center of New Eden.

And it sufficed as a life. For many years long after his mother's dinners of boiled rocks had burned the last of her pots, and long after his father's neck twisted and snapped in the belt noose of his own slinging and the bastard was spaded deeper than Adam's excrement, long after the Belvedere home went silent but for the rumblings in Kennesaw's gut and heart, it continued to suffice. Hunko in this long expanse learned to spend his days by Grunts Pond intent on his own business without questioning if every distant twig snap or sudden flutter signaled Kennesaw coming to join him. The markers in Nedewen Field doubled, tripled, far outnumbered the spaces still to fill. Farms once cropped crapped out. True lost more apple trees. The tree that felled the Drells was milled to the nub Kennesaw rests on.

Days begat years, and years pushed the limits of Kennesaw's universe. He filled himself to overflowing with more knowledge than the library at Alexandria could ever hope to contain, but what had started out an enterprise of distraction became itself an enterprise in need of distraction. For, as Kennesaw soon discovered, every advance he learned of became mired in complications from times back when, worlds thrived and fell, adventurers turned warriors, and mankind, for all its smarts, seemed never to move much further from its primal aggressions than a newborn from its need for teat. Learning for itself began to wear on Kennesaw; the violence he learned of in the world beyond his began to wear on him. Wars begetting wars. The violence in his own life—how had that come to call? He read Tennyson and Cowper and Hopkins and came to understand the blight man was born with and born for. But where were the birthday teas begetting birthday teas?

The innocence of an afternoon on the shore of Grunts Pond? Why were these not among life's must-knows? One can only escape so far by knowing the names of the continents and the planets, and poetry is a very weak aspirin when one learns from history that for every rhyming couplet there's yet another senseless Carthage, Antietam, and Corregidor, another Flummox, and yes, another Kennesaw.

AT HOME, AT THE HEEL END of each day, after so many years of this, in Kennesaw there grew a feeling stronger and more burdensome, a feeling of something insufficient in the unfolding of his actions, an emotion not thought through. Where he had found a world more suited to what his mind told his heart he wanted, his heart began a retaliation that Kennesaw was challenged to rebuff. Dusk treks home took to detouring from the insistent road to the dirt one to the path down to Grunts Pond, where quiet steps were careful not to snap twigs, and where in his stealth even birds were not moved to flutter. After full meals daily of religion and science and philosophy washed down with gulps of wars, and more wars and wars meant to end wars that only started new wars, Kennesaw's diet wanted for nourishment he could only get from one place, and so he began nightly to snack on the sight of Hunko from behind the rock on the pond's edge, feeding on the lad and his industry at hand, and the hand, and the heart, and never ever letting on that what they had had, had never truly ended.

20. LUDDY

MAWZ ENGERSOL WOULD BE remembered for a night
he couldn't undo, and Brisket Whiskerhooven would be
remembered for an intimacy too urgent to keep quiet,
but what would Luddy Upland be remembered for, if
anyone's to remember him at all?

Luddy Upland and Mawz Engersol might be remembered as friends like Carnival and Hunko might
be remembered as friends, or like Kennesaw and True
might be remembered as friends, or like True and
Jubilee might be remembered as friends. They might
even be remembered as better friends than Zebeliah and
Frainey might be remembered as friends (even though

no one can remember if Zebeliah was a Hackensack or a Whiskerhooven), or better than Frainey and Chippewa might be remembered as friends, and possibly likely in the end remembered as better friends than True and Threesie might ever be remembered as friends if indeed they ever were truly friends at all, for as everyone remembers befriending Threesie Lope was as reckless a pastime as cleaning a gun in the dark.

Luddy's friendship with Brisket Whiskerhooven (whom everyone remembers was indeed a Whiskerhooven if for that one good reathon) was a friendship that might have grown and adapted itself through the ages like a river settling into its own smooth groove through a valley, had Brisket not been swept up young in that second wave of the big fever, and it was the friendship that Luddy should be remembered for, but time has done its darndest to obliterate that friendship from memory. To recall Brisket at all is to recall him at Grunths Pond and to recall hith lithping grunt-outh of "Knotsthy!" on a nightly bathith. What has passed from common lore is the lisp's Luddy-link, for it was Luddy Upland whose suggestion it was that Brisket repeat the name Knotsy over and over in order to break him of his articulatory encumbrance.

Night after night on the shores of Grunts Pond, Luddy would whisper encouragement into Brisket's ear to put all of his urgent business into getting the correct pronunciation of Knotsy's name into his mouth while in his hands his urgency went to work. It was an enterprising attempt at solving a problem that had plagued the lad since his first uttered words, which were, according to his mother, the two favored words out of his father's mouth, which were, as all who recall can attest, two words often spoken as one, which were the word "horth" followed by the word "thit," which is, as some folk might agree, the very definition of a legend. But, alas, practical as Luddy's remedy was, repeating Knotsy's name over and over was not the problem-solver it was hoped. In fact, it only led to further complications no one could have anticipated. For able as Brisket proved to be at his urgent business, he never did succeed at getting his tongue out of Knotsy's S.

And that's all the story anyone remembers, if anyone remembers any of that story at all.

The friendship people are more inclined to remember if they remember any friendship is the friendship between Luddy and Mawz Engersol. You could say that Luddy and Mawz would be remembered as close friends. What you could also say is that while they would be remembered as close friends, proof of their close friendship wasn't something anybody remembered ever knowing. Luddy and Mawz, while close friends, were not friends as close as Mawz's papa, Bull, had been friends with his good friend, Remedial Bliss.

Luddy, unlike Remedial, was an able fellow who could roll his own rocks and till his own rows and seed his own beds and didn't need Mawz to step in and muck things up like Mawz's father had done and look where that got Mawz, no thanks.

Luddy was someone who was always around when a day came and when a day went. The lands his father, Pernicious, had scraped raw with an instinct for farming that would have better served him had he been a locust, Luddy spent the better part of his life reinvigorating with God spit and cowshit, and at their finest, it could be said that his lands yielded chervil and lovage like nobody's business. Chervil and lovage were not a crop business that served his toils well; you could say he was better at doing a thing than he was at thinking about why he was doing it, but the man had to be commended simply for doing his old man one better, which was to get his lands to grow something—anything—edible. It was a truism that he could boil chervil in water flavored with lovage, lay chervil raw and dirty on a platter and sprinkle it with lovage he dried and crinkled to bits between his rake-like fingers, gnaw on one of the umbels that grew hat-rack like from the umbelliferous chervil stalk and masticate it to swamp mud and just before swallowing, chomp a bit of lovage to season the mash of it and make it go down double-icky; all of that was true, all of that he did, but none of that mattered a burp because no one wanted to eat it, for to everyone else, rutabagas and sorrel are a tastier twosome than chervil and lovage, yet muck up Luddy's thinking with a truism like that his good friend Mawz Engersol wouldn't dare, having learned from his own father what putting yourself into someone else's business can lead to, no thanks.

What few recall is that it was Luddy who knew about the business with Cozy and Bull and how that stepped on the toes of Mawz's dance date with True; that Luddy also was the first to hear from Mawz about Bull Engersol's unfortunate tumble from his spooked horse and his head's unfortunate encounter with a rock; about Mawz's burying his father and burying him beneath the spooked horse that threw him (Mawz never said how he dealt with the horse, one just assumes it was an unfortunate encounter between the horse's head and a bullet); and it was Luddy years later who found Mawz on the mound that marked the spot where his father and the horse were hell-bound, and who decided to leave the bird-pecked remnants of his friend's body exactly as he found them—heart gone, eyes gone, skin flayed rare, and True's pink velvet ribbon clutched in his maggoty hand.

So a story is lived, so a story lives on. Etched on the living as acutely as those cold chiseled onto stone

markers like the ones all atilt in Nedewen Field. Had
the sight of Mawz on the ground there been its own
self-wielding cold chisel, it could not have imprinted
itself on Luddy any deeper or more permanently than
the vision itself did without benefit of tool or intent.
For years, Luddy carried that final sight of Mawz with
him into every room and every planted row. It entered
his house, it walked his fields with him, it settled down
beside him on the two-seater privy, and no amount of
lye could make it decompose. It was in every forkful of
chervil, every crinkle of lovage, to the point where he,
too, grew to hate their taste. It wasn't so much the eyes
gone plucked, or the bones of Mawz's ribcage gnawed
raw. What haunted Luddy was that half-blackened,
half-maggoty hand clutching that pink ribbon. A desire
so close to its intent, as insistent as a full moon crowding
through the curtains, but foiled at the very end by the
very heart it sought. And how he had left the decomposing body there as if it were an animal corpse he'd
come upon and not his friend who not so long ago had
wanted so to live. To have left that body there for the elements to have their way with was unfinished business
that rattled in Luddy's mind like a door on loose pins
and he could not stop its noise. Had he done in Mawz
himself, his regret would not have been any louder.

Yet, stories etched on the living as on stone, with
the wear-away of time come to fade, and as on the

worn-away markers all atilt in Nedewen Field, in time leave to those looking on only indecipherable indentations suggestive of a something, but not a specific someone; a what, but not a definable when; a was, but not a particular how. Such was the way the memory of finding Mawz lost its outward definitions on Luddy's person; in time his flinching at the smell of cooking flesh subsided, and he was able to contain his stomach when seeing others eat meat down to the bone, and he developed a numb kind of patience whenever the subject of Mawz and True was being opinionated on for the umpteenth time. Without stating his disgust for their insensitivity, he'd offer up an alternative for folks to chew on, one he knew would turn their stomachs as they were turning his: a wagonful of his chervil and lovage and he dared them to refuse. Up until that afternoon on the ridge Luddy was as happy as any to offer his two Indian heads on whatever grist was churning in the daily mill. But from that vision on, he taciturned inward, and rarely would he speak unless he was yelled out of his numbness. You could say that the Luddy Upland who oncewas was left to rot in that same sun as his close friend, Mawz Engersol, or at least he wished he had been.

Bearing Mawz's testimony to life's cruel turns, keeping it as hidden in his own conscience as Mawz kept himself hidden behind trees from True's eyes all those years, then keeping hidden the final sad bits of Mawz's sad end deep in his heart as if his heart were deep as a six-deep hole—Luddy carried all that business through his life faithfully, honorably and guardedly, until the sharp details of it in time wore smooth and indecipherable, and the indented facts of it pitted and turned to powder, and Luddy was left with not so much the story itself as he was with its heavy and very particular sadness, much like the smell of flesh in the air after the rotting of it is done.

Folks who did not fully understand his friendship with Mawz or know the history that Luddy took great care to conceal, looked on Luddy as a man simply grown sad with time, for time will do that to a man who doesn't have much of his own story to live. You cannot blame people for not seeing what they cannot see, even when what they cannot see is so present before them. In Luddy, what they could not see, though it was as evident as air in the lung, was that his sadness for Mawz, having taken up such prominent a place in his heart, *became* the story of his *own* life.

THINK OF LUDDY UPLAND and you think of labor and patience and steadfastness and chervil and lovage. His name is one of those names like Zebeliah Was-She-a-Hackensack-or-Was-She-a-Whiskerhooven (it no longer even matters that no one can remember which) or

Elementary Hurlbutt that always comes up in the back stories to memories, not because of any deeds that can be attributed to him, though we do know there were at least three (urging Brisket's "Knotsthy" and leaving Mawz all maggoty and growing crops everyone considered icky). More likely Luddy figures in the river of New Eden's narrative simply because he was one of any number of stones the waters rolled over on their way to somewhere more eventful; a life who, for all his life, breathed in and breathed out on a steady daily schedule during the moments when something special was happening to somebody else.

Think of Luddy Upland and the virtues of labor and patience and steadfastness—all serviceable virtues, nice to think about, but not a one of them strikes a representative image in the mind that you'd care to place on a pedestal or admire when painted on the blade of a saw. Virtue on its own, with no blocky shape to its head, or lanky carriage of its body, no hump that sets it apart or a third hand coming out of a hip, will not get you effigized in bronze and set down in the middle of town where it's an honor for eyes to ogle you and birds to cover your head and shoulders in feces. No one builds bonfires on a Saturday night to the patiently sturdy and silent. No walking stick is whittled to celebrate the slow-building, day-to-day steadfastness of nice and unassuming. And surely never was a sonnet composed that praised the heavens above-age for chervil and lovage. When you're in command of your own life but not commanding, and even though you are the first to think of others, you are not the sort whom others think of first. And everyone would have told you that about Luddy, if they'd remembered to.

HAD LUDDY UPLAND BEEN someone with a light in him he'd have dug a hole and given his friend his proper due. But all his life he felt the lack of something essential inside of himself, a specialness, a spark, an impulse that would lift him up from merely living to feeling himself alive. And whatever it was that was missing in him, he was convinced others could see.

He felt himself to be the woods at dusk, illuminated from beyond his edges by the pale glow that spilled off others and lit his underbranches in bits of afterglow. The flame he saw others burn with he could not for himself in himself spark with flint, and he so wished he had it in him to do. *If I only had a light in me,* he thought, *nothing blinding, nothing that would give the sun a run for its money or make the full moon feel inferior, a modest light would do,* he reasoned, *a pale star behind a star behind a star, a faraway dot that could light my own tiny orbit like a half-lit firefly, the tiniest sparkle that years from now might remind you, or you, or you, of me*—that's all he wanted in himself, but finding nothing in himself, he settled for the borrowed light of others by becoming the match that fused their way. He had urged Brisket to repeat a name while handy-Andying his urgent business and Brisket's not-so-silky recitation of that repetition forever became that lad's legacy. He'd stood steady-Luddy for Mawz to confide in, and carried his friend's secrets for him and took on his friend's sadnesses as deeply as any of his own he might have sunk under himself had he thought enough of himself to do so first, but in the end it did not make of him the lasting memory his labor and patience and steadfastness made of them. Tell Mawz's story without Luddy and the story has strength all its own; put Luddy in and he adds to it by not detracting from it. Brisket, though he will fade from memory like all the rest, a ghost's ghost in a ghost's story, doesn't need Luddy to hit the mark any more than Knotsy needed Brisket to wet her dreams. You don't remember the match that lights the fuse; you remember the bang.

WHO CHOSE THE ACRES of land where the end lasts forever? Luddy always wondered this about Nedewen Field. Was it a founding father who first toed a spade in the ground beneath the grasses to assess the ease of digging holes here? Or was it, perhaps, in an earlier time, from the time before the discovery of the already discovered, was it a tribal elder out seeking his own peace one day who came upon this place where the wind speaks in hushed tones and thought the spirits would find eternal ascendance here? Or was it a soul less advanced in a time more primitive who one day no more remarkable than any other in his still-forming world on this very spot stumbled onto his own loneliness under the wide open skies above here? Luddy liked to think it was this latter man, an earlier incarnation of his own unlit self. In Luddy's imagination he was a muted, though thoughtful spear-wielder, cousin perhaps to dweller or nephew or great-great-grandson, out exploring this very patch of land for whatever might be found here, when he came upon the carcass of a fellow spear-wielder so like himself, fallen and rotting in the afternoon sun, his spear still gripped in his maggoty hand. There was no other spear-wielder around, no beasts, the landscape had bubbled up only knee-high here so no ground nearby could provide any hiding; all there was was the unblinking sun in the sky above to know what felled this carcass and the sun wasn't saying.

This curious soul sniffed and poked and kicked that naked form so like himself for any signs of life in its limbs or any glint of light in its black-socket eyes, but found only lifelessness there in that form so like a rock now. Spear-wielder hadn't traveled to this spot with any companion, nor did he miss the company a companion might have provided. But coming upon this fallen form he felt for the first time a longing to not be alone. Warm as the sun was on his fur and skin he started to tremble at what he could not fully picture to be the state of his own next form; that the next form of himself might be that form on the ground, lifeless and rock-like and rotting. With this odd new dread of his own future state settled on his skin and fur as snug as any odor, he felt as never before his own nakedness to the unblinking eye of that afternoon sun, and for the first time ever in his tramp life reasoned that perhaps that eye knew something he did not. In his evolving understanding, he looked around his still-bubbling, still-hissing world, and it dawned on him that there might be in the vastness over his head a presence in that eye that he could not sniff nor poke nor kick, and to that presence spear-wielder attributed all that he did not understand. That presence would stare down upon him no matter what and see him for what he was, and it was that presence that would give him back license to be who he might have it in him to be. Spear-wielder looked at the fallen form and at his own not-so-fresh flesh, scanned the landscape for answers he knew he wouldn't find anywhere out there, then raised his eyes as much as he could to the sky, and then lowered them lower than the ground beneath his feet where a strange new sensitivity greeted them.

The rotting body was cold to the touch, but the

ground was as warm as the sky. And only by covering that lifeless form with the earth below him would spear-wielder cover his own nakedness to that eye in the sky above.

So unnamed spear-wielder, this faceless early man, this Luddy of the dawn, not really understanding what he was doing, he dug a hole by hand and he rolled the carcass into it, and the carcass landed with the spear still it its hand and most of its face face up, and the afternoon sun illuminated the black-socket eyes with a final twink of borrowed light and in those eyes unnamed spear-wielder, faceless early man, Luddy of the dawn, saw himself. Spear-wielder stood above the hole staring down at the carcass with unfinished thoughts about his own next form, and as he did, the sun began to settle behind his back, and the twink of borrowed light in the sockets of the carcass's eyes went back to their lender forever. And spear-wielder, he stood there a little longer feeling empty and not knowing why, then he knelt to the ground and scooped back into the hole the earth he had hollowed it of. The light had gone out of the form he found, and only by covering it from the light of day could he see his own way to this next form of himself.

In time, more holes followed more carcasses, and more pairs of hands than his own made ritual work of scooping and hollowing and rolling, of drying and wrapping, of dressing and boxing. From one observer grew small clusters standing shoulder to shoulder around the lifeless holes. In time the odd new sense of dread that made spear-wielder feel so alone that lone day swelled communal, and the small growing clusters who stood shoulder to shoulder around the lifeless holes felt their dread bind them heart to heart, united by a sense of something they could not sniff nor poke nor kick. They were naked as fur and skin to the vastness over their heads, and, in time, under their bonnets and boots, too, just as naked to that unblinking eye in the sky above. But united in their nakedness to that eye, they felt inexplicably warmed, or so they told themselves to keep the cold from returning.

BRUSH AWAY THE MOSS on any of the broken teeth markers in Nedewen Field and lay over the pocked stone surface a sheet of clean paper, then take a charcoal stick and rub it across the paper to reveal the faint etchings of names and dates underneath, and you'll find emerging from the pits and pocks many an Upland who came and went and left nothing of themselves more lasting than a weathered old stone in an overgrown field, naked and alone under that vast sky above, and Luddy is just one more among them. Hunko Minton found Luddy on the path side of the Upton side of Nedewen Field only a day or two after he must have fallen and failed, and Hunko thought it the right thing to do to drag Luddy's corpse inside the walls of Nedewen Field and dig a hole for his friend. There'd be no box; there was no point. It was a hot spring day and the sun was rushing the world to start anew, and he could already see on the lump in the grasses a picnic squirming. That sun in the sky wasn't doing his decomposing friend any favors.

21. TRUE

TRUE LAY IN HER BED in a vapor of smells, all hers. Coming from every opening, riding fluids of every consistency, insistent on getting out. There were odors from her bowels and from her bladder, odors from her mouth, her nose, her skin, even odors she hadn't happened upon since her rag days, all of them in a rush. Her body was letting go of the past.

She was a wet tangle of clothes on a larger frenzy of wet clothes that served as a mattress on her broken, sunken bed, the very bed in the very room in which her mother had labored her to odors and fluids of a different promise. The seepage must have started soon after she fell into slumber for she distinctly remembered squatting over her slop pot to do her nightly business before getting into bed and feeling so good that she'd emptied herself of so much. She'd long ago given up racing to her privy when the urge to empty rushed through her system. Too often on her way out of the house her body got ahead of her intentions and what she hoped to aim into the black hole out back trickled, seeped, spurted or gushed down the stairs, on the parlor's braided rug, in the kitchen, sometimes she left a trail running through the entire house, sometimes without her even realizing it. To remedy: she placed a bowl in every room, two in her bedroom (one of those was her washbasin), and when her body's immediacy came to call she had the answer for it handy. These bowls had saved her butt more than once, although she had to admit that in the past week or two, the immediacy had stepped up its insistence, and more than once she'd had to let go before she could even reach the nearest one. She felt the dampness all around her, some of it wriggled through her fingers like custard. Had she actually used the bowl last night, she wondered, or did she only dream it? Her thoughts, these days, like her insides, were loosening themselves and escaping her body. If she had only dreamt it, dear God that meant her body was going its own way in defiance of her also departing mind, and if that was the case, what was the point of making it to the day after today?

The odors and the fluids were mystery enough, but there was also a noise that she couldn't put her finger on. She'd only first been aware of it when she woke to her body's pre-dawn surprise, but as soon as she was awake and disgusted by herself, she was awake and disturbed by the indistinguishable sound, the slow over and over of it, a tap, syncopated as water dripping, only echoless.

Was it coming from close by or far away? She couldn't see anything in the dark and the sun wouldn't be up for hours. Outside on the roof? Inside of her head? The front door? A pot on the stove? A loose shutter? A stray thought? It was something coming from someplace, that tap, and if she didn't get up to find it she would surely go mad. If only it was a knock and not a tap. A knock wears its good shoes and its Sabbath face. A knock is a braggart who yells out, *I'm here*! You can confront a knock right away; make it state its business and go. But a tap is more of a child's game: it giggles, *Come find me*! A tap was something Threesie Lope would bedevil her with. *That Threesie*, she said to the vapor-filled darkness, *always needing to unsettle me just to make the wind blow!* The sound of her own voice was almost as unsettling as the tap. She hadn't uttered a word in days, not even to herself, not so much as *git!* to the raccoons that'd made a home in her pantry. Hearing her voice now it sounded so unimpressive—the smells were stronger; the tap was stronger.

214

Listening all morning and half the afternoon and finally she'd had enough. She gripped the headrail of her bed and pulled her wet self to her side; it was more of a struggle to force her legs over the edge and pull her wet self from there to sitting. She caught her breath, her feet didn't feel the grit on the floorboards yet, she inhaled her own musk deep and pushed herself off the bed to feel the floor at last, she felt a squish under her left foot (had she missed both bowl and bed?) and from stooping, slowly stretched herself out like a crumpled piece of paper unfolding to straightening out her creases as much as she could. In the time it took her to unfold out of bed and stand, apes had walked erect faster.

Tap.

Her hands were aching more than usual but she drew her wet cardigan as tight as her four good fingers and the one remaining button would allow, even though the hole she married it to was three holes too low. At least she was out of bed. There was a reason for her to get out of bed today, if only she could recall it; the days when she had a reason grew fewer and fewer. She searched the room for the reason but it must have been off playing the same hiding game with the noise. She pushed a wild branch of her gray nest to the crown of her head and secured it with a laundry pin she'd fumbled for and found next to the pruning shears on the bedside table, and tired as she was she resolved to go downstairs and find the noise and give it breakfast and maybe then it would be on its way. She nudged aside the night's unused soil bowl with a bare blue foot and followed an ancient path out the doorway that hadn't had a door on it since Cozy's drinking days, and as she descended the stairs in the dark she let the treads guide her squeak by squeak.

Tap.

The sound was all around her in the air. A right turn at the bottom of the S-curved run where the last tread was worn to a lopsided frown, through the narrow path in the clutter in the dining room with its dangling distraction in the center over the table, and into the kitchen, she followed the sound and the sound followed her like two clouds of dust in a foot race.

Maybe she was just hearing things because she hadn't slept for years, not real deep sleep, not really. Real deep sleep for True was the only store in town worth shopping at, and it stopped doing business with her long ago. Every day now she felt tired and she looked tired and she moved tired and she ate tired and she saw tired and she certainly smelled tired and now she heard tired, too. There was no way to tell anymore if the fatigue that chewed through her walls and moved into her body like the raccoons did in her pantry was due to a lack of proper slumber or an excess of years. Her spine this morning couldn't remember its purpose for the day any better than she could, and searching for an answer it curled her torso into a question mark, which asked her the most basic question of all: *why are you still alive?*

Tap.

The same stray branch of her nest she mashed before she mashed up from her face again and as she did she searched the room with pleading eyes: *where was that damned noise coming from?* She'd believe anything that might swat the noise from her head. But neither the ice-box nor the eggbeater said boo.

A few things grab hold in the dark—the best is fire. For a moment, an ancient tug in True knew to kindle a few twigs in her cooktop, and when she struck the match and the dried sticks ignited, cavemen came alive. She stood among them entranced; staring into the blue-orange-yellow unknown like it was the first flame ever. The moment lasted as long as the stick fire licked, but the flashes shrank to little bubbles of flame then a glow spot then a puff of smoke and it was over, the fire letting go of itself, leaving a trace of woody after-smell, not as stenchy as True's, and True's transfixion puffed out itself and she remembered what brought her down-stairs to begin with: the tap. Only now, it wasn't a tap, it was a knock.

Knock.

She had preferred a knock to a tap only a while ago, but now that she had it she could kick herself. One good thing: she could at least tell where this noise came from. The new sound was issuing from the outer door of her front vestibule and as she held her breath and listened, oh Lord, the timbre of it became abstractly familiar. It reminded her of that most annoying howdy-do of a knock that's the stock in trade of Kennesaw Belvedere. *What's he doing here?* she asked a spot over there.

If Kennesaw Belvedere wasn't her oldest friend AND her cousin AND maybe even her uncle AND possibly her half-brother (it wouldn't surprise her), AND one of the only living souls left in town, she'd have nothing to do with the man.

Knock.

She listened once with her jaw thrust towards the sound, she squinted and listened twice with her shoulder leading the way, and when she was sure she was sure that *this* sound was Kennesaw's damnably familiar howdy-do of a knock and she wasn't imagining it any more than she wasn't imagining the tap and was resigned to letting him in, she moved an empty pot onto the snuffed-out flame of her cooktop, and told the kettle to watch it, then made her way out of the kitchen and into the dining room and nudged aside a stack of berry hallocks on the buffet and answered her breakfront.

She told her grandmother's blue-and-white transfer-ware dishes to come in, and when the dinner plates decorated with old sailing vessels and the quarter inch of dust on them didn't budge, she said to the rubber boot on the broken chairback on the dining table that she had no use for fools who didn't know their own mind, and old age was no excuse. *C'mon in Kennesaw,* she said to an apple basket, *hang your hat there,* and she chinned to a plant stand on which sat a pot of bent gray stalks. Then pointing a shaky elbow at a raccoon trap she had once mistaken for a slop bowl told her guest to follow her into the privy and bring the tray with the paint and mind the squirrels.

Don't take all of my time, she said to the grandfather clock in the hallway as she led her mute guest first into the nook beneath the stairs where she paused for a confused moment before the heavy black telephone on the small clamshell shelf (it used to ring two-long for Bliss and three-short for Lope in days long forgotten), then past the front vestibule where no one would be coming to call for hours, then into her front parlor where dust and cobwebs and feed bags and egg crates and half-filled slop bowls warmed in the afternoon sun. Somewhere over her shoulder True said, *Sit your ass down in the good chair,* and nodded her nest in the direction of the firebox full of brambles.

Knock.

The sound confused her now. Here was Kennesaw, that knock was his, so whose knock was it? She didn't want her confusion in the same room as Kennesaw; he had always looked to her for wisdom after all, so she guffed to keep her guest from guessing. *That's just porcupines*, she said in a mad rush of breath, looking first out the south-facing parlor oriel, then under the davenport. *What a damn bother they are at our years!* she remarked. She asked the woodstove, *How many is it now, Kennesaw?* but a woodstove never reveals its age. *Such a bashful one*, she said, and kicked a small striped tuft of fur that had desiccated itself on her parlor's braided rug who knows when. *Let's see*, True said. *I'm older than apple cider and your mother was a butter churn and the winter Grunts Pond caught on fire there were only six days when laundry needed ironing, so that means you must be at least as old as your first pair of overalls and I was a mere slip of a girl when you fumbled to button those straps for the first time, so that makes you at least ten to fifteen miles shorter than me, give or take a postage stamp.* The woodstove having become a stack of fruit crates said neither nay nor yay, which was all the silence True needed to know her calculations were somewhere in the barn if not directly in the corncrib. *It's all pennies and pins*, she said, with a laugh that didn't want to be funny, *aren't they such a drawer full of nonsense? Birthdays? You've lost weight, Kennesaw*, she said to the candlestick lamp, *stop hovering and sit down and quit your tomfoolery.* She lowered her own bony hips to the stack of egg crates in front of the davenport, the crates having retained their wooden form while the davenport and its springs and horsehair stuffing had exploded the worn velvet fabric from within. Good thing there were as many old, soiled clothes piled on it as on her bed to soften things, or a sitter wouldn't be able to stand it. She braced her descent with a hand on a mound of pine-cones in a skillet and informed her guest, *This upholstery is Mother's favorite. By the way, I didn't bake an ice wagon. Who needs ants?*

Knock.

The sound was as persistent as a leaking roof but she didn't want Kennesaw to think she was hearing nois-es because he'd be sure to tell Loma Soyle who'd tell her sister Petie who'd tell Jubilee Aspetuck who'd tell Frainey who'd tell Chippewa who'd tell that Herkimer Minton who'd tell Luddy who'd tell Mawz, and if Mawz Engersol heard that she was a girl as unsound as the sound around her was unseen, he wouldn't come to her house tonight to take her to the dance and if she didn't dance with him tonight she'd just *die!*

GONE FROM TRUE'S DAY-TO-DAY now was her impend-ing one hundred years, her numb left hand, history as she lived it, and the word *tomorrow*. Gone was the stone she had made of her youthful fancy, pulverized back to its volcanic state of forming, pliable once again to her desires. In place of it all was Kennesaw taking up her time in the parlor when she should be upstairs prettying her girlish self for the arrival of the boy of her dreams.

The tap was back now. She hadn't noticed it gone until its return where it united with the knock. It must have gone out to run an errand when she wasn't listening.

The tap, the knock, Kennesaw—how impatient she was with them all. She waited a polite span of time for Kennesaw to grow bored with their visit and offer his fare-thee-wells and leave, but when the firebox neither cleared his throat nor slapped his hand on the davenport's arm, when the only sound in the room was from the wind riffling the decayed last shreds of a lace curtain that hung over the open parlor oriel like a veil torn from a bride, True groped the musty air for a final say on the subject, not that she could recall what subject was in the air.

Knock.

Tap.

There are fewer stars in the skies over New Eden than there were when I was a girl, she said to the portrait of her great-great-grandfather, Remedial Bliss, the first of the Remedials, although the man with the bloodshot nose was too preoccupied with a bow saw and a cluster of rhubarb to take a whack at the subject. *Have you noticed that, Kennesaw? Have you ever tried to count them, one by one?* She was looking up at her parlor ceiling now with its water stains and buckled plaster and millions of crackled paint peelings that had been there since before there was a before—the thousands hanging on and the thousands that had already let go. From the sunlight filtering in through the oriel window the tips of the peelings caught intermittent flashes, so that even during the day her parlor made a night of it.

Knock.

Tap.

She shook her head free of the sounds but what she really loosed were stars, and as her head bobbled a large flake of paint fell out, and, riding the flake as one might a shooting nova down the blueish white of her neck and onto the frayed grays of her cardigan was a mud-dark potato bug, its long legs frantic to grab hold of anything not transitory. *I used to try to fit all the stars in my saltshaker, all those stars, all those damn stars, but they gave me gas,* True confessed to her guest. As the words were coming out so, too, were the sounds again, and again, and again, knock-tap, knock-tap, the syncopated dripping water dripping faster. She was growing frayed as her cardigan, eager to push the whole stray branch of the day away with a wave of an arthritic fist.

Surely the accumulated wonder of her musings had distracted Kennesaw and rendered him speechless, for once again she heard nothing from him, and hearing nothing, was gratified because she was tiring at a gallop and had nothing more to add. She decided now was the moment to pour the tea, maybe he'd leave after she did, so she reached for the slop bowl atop the Good Book that lately made a better cuspidor than a doorstop and tipped it in a tremulous arc, letting the pale yellow fluid splash onto her lap and down her legs and puddle on the dirty braided rug, where it took its time to seep in and left a wide ring of wet. Her head was still in the stars, and quite a few stars were still on her head. She asked her guest to remind her what he took in his long johns. She was working so hard to keep herself focused and keep the noises at bay. On the count of knock, tap, shrug, True reached a trembling hand inside of her cardigan and removed a withered flap and told the bookcase it could pour its own damn paint. *Drink up!*

Knock.

Tap.

The knock was overpowering, the tap the last straw. The two sounds had fused together like a shot and echo—knocking-tapping, knocking-tapping—coming at her as a wide flank firing, knock-tapping, knock-tapping, knock-tapping, and the force of the hits was great enough to blast this present imagined moment from her consciousness and land her smack down into the one she had waited her whole life to begin.

It was on a summer breeze that True floated like an airborne ribbon from the parlor through the foyer back to the cluttered dining room and into her dream. Her young man, Mawz Engersol, had stepped through the breakfront and was waiting for her in the air over the trash-topped table; nothing else on the ceiling tantalized her with visions of the life she'd have ahead as much as the single incandescent bulb that was hanging by a twig of wires from above like it was the last lone apple on a tree that would yield no more. True circled the table in a skip-to-my-Lou, she dipped her eyes and fluttered lashes she no longer grew, she pinched the hems of a skirt only Mawz could have seen and twirled amid the chaos with increasing breathlessness keeping time, the knock and tap in her chest forced her to stop, and she swooned and the room swirled on, and smelling sweet jack-in-the-pulpit over her own foul air she smiled a girl's most important smile at the suitor who smit her, and smoothed a pink velvet memory with a numbed, gnarled fist, and looking that unlit bulb in its long-ago disconnected eyes she uttered the answer that would have lit up her life:

Oh Mawz, she said, her words halting and breathy as forward they looked to their end, *you most certainly, may have, this dance.*

22. Knotsy

BETWEEN THE FULLNESS OF YOUTH and the frailty of old age stretched a breadth of years full of aimless wandering. We were told that in this time joys and sadnesses would come at us as gently as spring rains and as savage as winter howlers, sometimes out of season in their volleys, but always one in succession of another. We were told we would weather them one at a time with no sense of the next one on its way, believing this one is the great one, the love, the laugh, the start of something new, or that one with its grief and throbbing loss is the one we won't outlive. They would come at us, these highs and lows, when we were in our highs or lows, and we must find the strength to face them one on one, one after another, and we must live them as they come, and outlive them as they go, and get through them and to the other side as well as we can, for these years can last far longer than a body can stand them. But stand them is what we are born for.

We could not imagine these years when young. Youth is too busy inventing itself to bother with the basics everyone older knows already. We were told from our earliest times that the greatest bulk of our years must be a solitary pursuit, each one of us alone in our own bed, our names spelled out with the last letters, our hearts the last beating organs, because our blood had trickled too thin into a puddle in the middle of town and the puddle at long last was going dry. All around us were the tadpoles of warning born in that withering wet spot—the bodily extras and absences, the eccentricities and melancholia; they sprouted bowlegs and short little arms and hopped about with their admonishments that we must forego all fairy-tale desires, for all we'd give birth to from our loins if we should hop on one another would be frogs. We listened. We were not blind. It was obvious that the inbred Minton sniffer would look more apt were it protruding from the keel of a boat. Or Lopes from loins less polluted might not have come out in a litter so overwrought and underwhelming. But oddnesses like these surely are the low-hanging fruit that suffers because it does not get the sun in all its glory, and we young and hardy would climb to the top of the tree and pick the best and prove the past wrong.

We were of a mind that the old were too old to remember youth bursting through its pants or the yearning one feels for a wooden doll to squirm itself human; and that the older were already of an old world that in its unincandescent, unhydrolic, unpetroleumed way would never understand what youth now knew to do. Each one of us with our urgent business in our hands, or with our skirts up in a tumble and the grasses tickling our ever-mores: we'd climb our nimble way farther up than our elders to the top of the tree and gorge ourselves on the pick of the crop in that glowing sun, and with our stamens put to pistils there would not come a mutant among us. We were young, and that's what we believed.

In that youthful time of self-invention, we judged our swellings and emissions as the sole of life's sum. We were the first galleons to cross the oceans and discover this new world of fervent urgency. We could see the distant lands and all the lush new growth where we would put in at the end of our journey, and we could smell the earthy air blowing across the waters to meet us, and in its thrall, we would need no sextant to guide our ships to port. The Cozy Blisses among us shot their cannons across our bows to sink our expeditions before they ever left the shores of Grunts Pond, and we only shook our heads in amused pity at their outdated warnings and old-fashioned weapons. Surely they had forgotten, if they'd ever known at all, the pinch and struggle of skin engorging in tight denim and what it meant to free it and let it run wild where it wanted to run wild. If they'd ever known at all they would not have pointed knuckleless fingers at the epidemic of humps and carbuncles, or preached themselves purple inveighing against the home-grown blight that had obliterated family after family. Had they ever felt what we felt they would not have been so adamantine that we should learn to live with that swelling turning blue, they would recall the twitch and sting and ache and soften to our stiffness and send us seamen off on our white-capped voyage with a robust shanty singing *go forth and mutate!* But they did not, and we begrudged them for it.

We all of us swollen and alone chose to hold out until the old were no more, and once they were gone we could let go. But we were growing up, we were swelling to our peaks, holding out was getting harder and harder, the sweat of impatience was beading up on the tip of us, we were each of us a Carnival yearning to go the full three-ring circus on every Jubilee; the old were dropping like overripe fruits from untended trees and soon every one of them would be rot and rum and once they were we could open the spigot of our longings. We were so close, and we might have gone all the way, had that flopping flounder Knotsy O'ums not scared every last one of us limp.

Knotsy's birth was maturity's first slap in our collective faces that maybe the old folks were on to something. The spoiled fruit of Butte and Columbine's cousinly loins was born with not enough skin and too many seeds, as pale and permeable as a jellyfish. She was alive as a barnacle is alive, sticking to life more than living it, and while she had most of the right body parts in a few of the correct places that evolution decreed, the functions they performed were throwbacks to that oceanic era just before fish walked on land. To those of us who were but a moonlit night away from our maiden voyages to that new land we thought we were the first to discover, the moonlight shining clear through Knotsy's filmy flesh like the brightest lighthouse beacon cautioned our ships from anchoring off that shore. The warnings that had taken mis-shape only here and there, on Knotsy were in full mis-formation, and we came as almost one to the understanding that this was what so many generations of cousins on cousins had come to—a weakened, watery fluid with no more life to it than the algae on a still pond; and the likelihood of any two of us bringing forth another one of her was a shallow shoal full of sharp rocks and certain peril. From there on out, almost every bit of urgent business stayed a ship on the water going nowhere.

BUT URGENT BUSINESS UNADDRESSED undoes. We were told from our earliest times that the greatest bulk of our years must be a solitary pursuit, and we came as almost one to understand the wisdom of this, but not a one had wise words to offer on what to do with all that urgency that would not abate, wisdom come nothing. We graduated from our youth into our adult years with this unspent urgency pent to implosion, and only on the shores of Grunts Pond or in the tickling grasses on Tumblers' Ridge did any of us rid ourselves of the urges as a oneman ship of its ballast; but always the urges flooded back in and filled us with their distracting vigor and we would have to rid ourselves again, from fill to rid, fill to rid, nothing coming of our urgency but more urgency— urgency with nowhere to go. Urgency with nowhere to go is life in a suicide cycle.

Urgency had given New Eden years and years and years of life, but that life with us would end. We came as almost one to accept that a ship with too much ballast will at last sink under its un-unloaded weight, and one by almost one we did. The urges that had set sail on the shores of Grunts Pond and in the tickling grasses on Tumblers' Ridge with no focused port, no shore in sight, only horizon and more horizon on the horizon, swamped us each and almost every. We wandered through our days in motion devoid of purpose, making do with our tasks, our needs, but without plans for making do again until it was time to make do again, repeating our days only because they repeated themselves. And this was how the desires for cousin on cousin as the years began to pass grew fewer and fewer, and with it the need for heart to heart grew less and less, and as urgency subsided to pastime and pastime became part of the past, the fluids we no longer needed dried to crust. There was nowhere to set sail for and no longer a reason. And we almost all of us sank to the murky bottom of life where loneliness doesn't know what to do with itself.

This is what our middle years were made of: loneliness, stretching out a land bridge from the fullness of youth to the frailty of old age, day after day after day. Each and almost every one of us rode through these years as a barnacle on a hull, sticking to life more than living it, enacting the making do that makes up a life. We had our crops to tend, our chores, our mending, trees to fell and, when we fell, our holes to dig, and we did all of this as best we could as weather and wherewithal allowed. We had our Sunday Sit Downs and our tumblings; the Drells had their walkabouts, the Lopes their nightly howlings. The world around us modernized and moved ahead, and in small ways we let the modern world fill us with its urgency—its amps and volts, its rotary dials, the chug-a-lugs that did our farm work for us. But as the modern world around us moved ahead faster and further, we almost all of us in our own time unsuctioned from the hull of that progression. The sagging wires that had been strung from pole to pole down the center of town like a slack stitch through a temporary hem we were not sorry to see removed when the main road was forked at both ends, leaving the stretch in between unneeded. Like the main road through town with no destination up ahead we were unrouted from the voyage that is life, and no illumination stronger than a candle's cast is needed when there's nothing much to look for and nowhere to go in the dark.

Some of us were castaways together. Petie Soyle had Loma to light her way through these dark years, and all three Lopes had each other, despite each one's frequent desire to rid herself of the other two. They were all to each of their siblings a ready presence that would serve the need for simple companionship in the daylight, or be a voice that called back in the dark when the night was too long to go through alone. In sibling-ness these five had a built-in buffer to unrelenting silence, but as they found—as we all found—noise alone was not enough of a comforting touch.

Urgency wants what it wants beyond mere want. And what it wants most of all is more than an echo, more than a shadow, more than the frictive slip of flesh in flesh. It was in our middle years that we came to understand that the distant shore we thought in our youth we would be the first to discover was not in fact urgency's final destination. That land, out past where we could see ahead on the horizon, was but a barrier island off the coast of the real shore to be landed on—the land beyond the biological, far removed from the urgent, the undiscovered world where exists the deepest urgency of all: to attach one's lonely fate to another's. This is the real land bridge of life—the land bridge between birth and eternity.

BUILD A BRIDGE, build a box, in the end it's all the same.

From the time Hunko Minton first gripped a hammer with as much authority as he gripped himself, it was his job to build the town its boxes. He'd measure the body's height for the box's length and the spread of its shoulders for width; when rigor mortis set in and the ankles froze forever and made its feet stick straight up, he'd measure their length and that would determine how tall the box should be. Only once in his box-building life did he ever take an unorthodox measurement to build an unorthodox box, and that box was the box he built for his own father, and for that box he measured his father's stiff Minton sniffer and that sniffer sticking straight up was taller by far than his stiff Minton feet, so Hunko cut a hole in the lid of his box and added a rectangular ell to the face of it like a rectangular branch growing off of a rectangular tree, and it made that box the only add-on box Hunko ever built in his life. The only box that would have ever rivaled it was a box that was never built, and that box would have been the last box Hunko ever built, and had that box ever been built, that box would have been his own.

He was good at building rectangles, not bad at toe-pinchers, too. His measurements were always nearly perfect; he'd take them once and never felt the need to take them again. He'd cut his planks—the same size for the lid as the base, the same size for the sides, the same size for the head and the foot. He never worried about boxes needing a lining, nor did he build them with any thought to comfort. If, when nailed together, the box proved too snug for its occupant because his measurements were a couple of inches off, rather than start from scratch he'd bust a couple of bones and make the body fit.

No sanding, no planing, no tongues in grooves, no chamfered edges. Nothing fancy was ever needed for something the occupant would never see. Hunko's one concern was durability. Hardwoods make the longest-lasting boxes; cherry and walnut and oak assure eternity. The sound of his hammer hitting the nails that nailed the boxes shut as it echoed across the valley was the boarding call of that eternal journey readying to launch, and like a ship's horn or a train's whistle, if you heard it, it meant one less person you'd ever see again.

As the middle years thinned New Eden of its remnants, Hunko built the boxes that sent almost all of us on our way. He boxed up Frainey Swampscott in a cherry toe-pincher, and sealed her up with Chippewa's hard-gristled heart in her hands. Zebeliah Was-She-a-Hackensack-or-Was-She-a-Whiskerhooven became twice the woman she ever was in her final days, swelling up like a summer melon, so Hunko made for her a walnut rectangle as wide as a wagon. (It was equal in width to the doublewide he'd built all those many years ago for Russett and Circe Aspetuck.) Though Luddy Upton had no box at least Hunko dug him a hole; there would be neither box nor hole for Petie and Loma Soyle, who were left to hold each other's hands until their hands turned to dust in the beds in the small room of their house where the tree limb came to fall and their days came to an end. Onesie Lope went the year of the walnut blight so she was evermored in oak; Twosie would have preferred oak herself but cherry was all there was, and because she did not like confinement in any form (something that must have had to do with being sandwiched in the middle of the trio in her mother's crowded womb), Hunko kindly gave her the first look at whatever lay ahead by fitting her lid with a window.

Threesie lived as long as cantankerous does, outliving both her sisters with a willfulness to experience life all alone, even if alone meant she'd be screaming for three. For her box Hunko reused scavenged soft planks of pine and poplar and ash and tulip he tore up from the floor and walls of the Lope family home. The planks were all irregularly lengthed, no two alike, and with arthritis stiffening his sawing arm and his hammering arm, to save that arm for his preferred activity he neither sawed nor hammered hard those planks to make a form at all. Instead, Threesie Lope traveled to wherever in a box one could hardly call a box; lumber rushing down a flooding river and coming to rest in an angry jumble of jagged boards and splintered planks all juts and edge roughs would be elegant joinery compared to what he mish-mashed up for her.

But for the mish-mash of fish and flesh that was the see-through Knotsy O'ums, Hunko took his greatest care of all, and made for her neither a rectangle nor a conventional toe-pincher to last in the dirt forever; instead he made her a seaworthy vessel to return her to her aqueous origins. No ordinary measurements would have served to make a box of any suitable proportions for the girl; for Knotsy never was at any one time in her brief life a height or width one could count on. Her fluid body, lacking in any discernible skeletal understructure, was a membranous mass ever in motion; when she walked she moved in a series of undulations and jumps similar to a salmon perpetually spawning upstream; at rest, her body appeared to loosen its tenuous hold on structure all together, turning as quivery and wobbly and runny as an aspic on a warm day.

It was wintertime, the winter of the silent ice, the year when snowy rain was all that fell and it froze on contact with every post and twig, every barn and barrel, every exposed bit of flesh that wasn't kept buttoned up; it was in this winter when Knotsy's life fluids froze and ceased forever. She was found by Hunko down by the frozen shores of Grunts Pond, hard as any fish you'd catch in fall and freeze for a meal much later in the year. Hunko was down there for his daily ritual, doubly urgent in his urgency to keep his unbuttoned bit of flesh from turning as sleek and hard as an icicle in his hand. Across the pond on the spot where Brisket Whiskerhooven undertook to strengthen his tongue on Knotsy's name all those years ago, Hunko spotted the tongue twister herself, a frozen lump, as shimmery as an egg white, encased in a veil of ice. It was uncommon for Hunko to ever interrupt his urgent business before his business was complete, but spotting Knotsy on that spot he cold-froze in his motions, and consequently, his hand cold-froze to his manhood. He was frozen this way when he crossed the frozen pond to study her frozen form, and frozen this way as he stood above her in his studies. Remembering Brisket's words, Hunko did what he needed to do to unstick the moment from his mind and his frozen hand. It was the first and last time in his life that anyone but Kennesaw ever inspired him to such an ending. And although it did the trick, whenever he thought back on this moment in his life, grunting *Knotsthy!* was the one memory he couldn't really warm to.

Perhaps it was the ice at hand that gave Hunko the idea to return Knotsy to the waters she was suited for. The ground was too hard to dig a hole, and would not be soft enough to do so until long after the first thaw of spring. But the ice on Grunts Pond would give way on its own when the sun came out of its winter hibernation. There'd be no digging to do; in fact, there'd be no need to make a box that would last any longer than a log submerged. So with pine and hemlock and balsam and spruce Hunko fashioned for Knotsy a kind of sarcophagus canoe, tapered at the head and tapered at the toe, with a lattice lid and a flat-bottomed hull. The lack of structure to her limbs came in handy when Hunko needed to snap both her frozen feet parallel to her ankles in order to make her head fit fully at its end.

The day Knotsy was to set sail it was too cold out for most to say their farewells. She had been the caution that came between urgency and eventuality for every member of the last of the last, and though she was not to blame for the rule that had sentenced us all to our solitary lives, the fact of her had made her an outcast the whole of her brief, transparent existence. She had clung to life like a barnacle, like us—alive but not really living. She breathed, she moved, she went through her days as a being with a pulse, yet without purpose, and we could see in her all too clearly the unlived lives we all had led. Perhaps to say good-bye to her was to say it to ourselves, and it was just too chilly a day to do that too soon.

Hunko slid her vessel out across the ice to the center of Grunts Pond, in view of Brisket's shoreside perch, and there it would sit for more than two months before it settled and submerged into the icy waters when they were finally ready to receive her in the exact same spot where all those generations ago Hezekiah Minton became the first New Edener to go beyond to forever. It will never be known how Knotsy felt about being Brisket's urgent inspiration. She never did in her time among us utter a word more solid than a bubble of spit. Yet, knowing the charity that in the recesses of every private heart forgives what it cannot help itself to begrudge, it is certain that the collective hope among us all is that Brisket's moonlit grunts all those years ago made Knotsy's fishy innards wriggle. And too, the hope that there would be for her a journey to complete what on dry land had eluded her. From there in the middle of Grunts Pond she could see the distant shore where Brisket once had called her name and with it still in the air she would need no sextant to guide her to his port. And if the vessel Hunko crafted for her didn't get her there, she could always swim.

23. KENNESAW

FROM HIS FATHER'S GROPES Kennesaw had run his shame to True as refuge, and later, with Hunko too bright an ember in his furnace and him dousing the flames in an education that ceased to distract him, True had been the keeper of Kennesaw's secrets, not that his secrets, she told him time and again, were anything to fault. In the years to come it was loneliness forged of shared grief and longing that drew Kennesaw to her; and finally, what kept him coming to her house for his birthday tea year after year was friendship based on age and familiarity, and the habits we can't shake and the hurts we can't outrun, and the senility that in its arbitrary mercy blocks our memories of it all.

As the wind picks up and the sky grays over, Kennesaw trudges the remaining miles into town, catching his breath by the hole in the stone wall at Nedewen Field where dust returns to dust. He passes the broken stone markers that show their old age like chipped teeth in a mouth full of mourning, and lays to rest the memories of those who have gone before him. He continues on down the gravel road and crosses the tangled patch that had once been the village green, and past the strip of acre beside the barn behind True's house where the prized row of Granny-Macs once stood.

It's taken him all of the morning and most of the afternoon and much of the last ninety-nine years to reach here. The weather is due to turn calamitous. Kennesaw runs a moist hand across his moist scalp as he continues on his way to True's. He approaches her plain front gate where he rests a moment before starting up again and making his way up her walkway and onto her front stone slab, which is only a pebble more settled than his.

One arm pumping and then the other. One leg shuffling and then the other. One ache and then another and then another and then another. And this is how the aged walk into heaven.

He's ninety-nine. It's been a long journey. Tea sounds good to him.

NOTHING IN LIFE ever really goes into a hole in the ground as long as there's a body that remembers, and as long as that body has breath in it, those rememberings join hands with time as it trudges to its indeterminable end, just as dirt caked and dried on an uncleaned spade joins with new dirt dug from a new hole, ground by a heel that tracks dirt of its own. And not until that heel has stepped its last, and the spade is dropped by the last hand to hold it in place and left to idle and rust in the dust with no one to make use of it ever again, does a remembering get forgotten for good.

A man can go crazy with thoughts of this ilk scurrying around his head like squirrels in an attic. Yet heady thoughts like these are typical for Kennesaw. Just before he stamped the mud off his boot heels on True's front porch, which was just before he felt the crack of his pants for any telltale wet spot of sting turned itch turned sticky, which was just before he rap-rappety-rap-rapped on the etched glass of her vestibule door, which was just before the door creaked open on its own as if on haunted hinges, he reminded himself that True with her senses gone to applesauce was lucky to no longer remember anything more puzzling of her own life than a few random pennies and pins in a drawer full of non-sense. Ninety-nine years were behind Kennesaw just as surely as the afternoon sun was well over his left shoulder and had burned a red ring round his nape. And just as sure as he'd track into True's house warm, dense crescents of clay, he'd muddy up her parlor with all his ninety-nine years full of living past, all his family shame and all his Hunko regret, and they'd push aside True's living past that she keeps in a mound of musty intimates, piled on the tattered davenport where she once sat waiting for Mawz Engersol to take her to a dance, and all of them can reminisce about the lives they didn't live at their annual how-do-and-happy-birthday. To have memories that make no sense, or ones that allow no peace, is bedevilment either way, and some merciful heel or hand might earn its entry into heaven by cleaving both their skulls with a spade.

It's so like Kennesaw to think this way that it's not surprising that as soon as he blinked his way into True's dark vestibule and juddered past a stack of wood crates over to her tattered parlor davenport and moved her musty intimates off the davenport and down onto a splotch of what smelled like fresh pee on the clay-hued hooked parlor rug, and finally sat his stinging, itching, clogged-up ass down on the tatters and felt a buckled spring where you don't readily invite a buckled spring, that the squirrels in Kennesaw's attic went frantically in search of nuts, and his bluer-than-blues lollopped, and his wits blew south, and in no time at all, face first into the musty mound of intimates atop the splotch of fresh pee on the clay-hued rug, Kennesaw and the clarity of his memories, in a fit of the vapors, landed.

24. Hunko, True, Kennesaw, Carnival, Jubilee, Luddy, Mawz, Zebeliah, Petie, Loma, Frainey, Chippewa, Knotsy, Cozy, Bull, Russet, Circe, Dweller, Spear-Wielder, Lak'isha, and Kip

So much of life happens in a house across town, on the other side of a closed door, in a room where we are not. From our vantage point beyond the place where life is happening to someone not us, we may hear of but not actually see the tumult as it plays out between husband and wife, father and son, sister and brother, sister and sister, girl and goat, friend and friend, stranger and stranger, chromosome and chromosome; the words we imagine shot and shot back may make our jaws unhinge and our eyebrows ripple in reaction to something we don't even know is true; the hits and hits back, if there are any, at the very least give our hearts a contrapuntal beat; and every so often, loathe as we are to admit it, the kiss and kiss back that we are certain of even in the absence of any proof will flow an envious blush to our faces that streams all the way up from our loins.

This is where the end begins.

By 2:46 EVERY MOLECULE in the heavens was marshaled to shove the sun where the sun wasn't ready to go, giving porch chimes the jitters like so many shrieking carillons, and even the leaves that weren't so ready to call it a season let themselves loose. Fly on by they did, airborne crisps, with their rheumatic touches of red and gold and edgings already drying to brown, past Hunko as he stormed the apple stumps behind True's house, the twelve trees now down to none, and into True's side yard and right under her south-facing parlor oriel all flush with his own autumn indignation.

ALL MORNING AND THROUGH much of the day the sky had allowed nothing more robust than a milky wisp to cross its brow. But at 3:15 cloud blasts dense as herds of crows spread to a great blush of black. Darkness of the kind only bats learn to love leached overhead and swallowed all movements on the ground in one long gulp. And before anyone could pack it a hamper for its travels, what was left of the sun was marked a pigeon and given the steel toe out of town.

By 3:20 grackles that had gathered on True Bliss's ridge beam began to grouse and mutter about the engulfing gloom, riffling their wings in annoyance with each impetuous breeze, and by 3:32 when the temperature took a swan dive, they got the jumps and fled north in a clash. Birds up above and Hunko a good head down below True Bliss's south-facing parlor oriel, not seeing up into the window exactly but not about to take flight. If only he had a bird's eye view through that air-bubbled window glass to the shenanigans he was certain of inside.

At 3:33, True's tattered parlor curtains took a sudden billow out the oriel's open center window then gasped back in. Hunko jumped up best his bowlegs would let

him, which was only about an inch, so he barely cleared
the drip edge below the bay and had no clear shot to
anything inside. Just then, the devil threw a lemonade
social and sent out for ice. It was the sound first that
hit him, then the sting on his skin, then the pounding
ouch of it. Hail as hard as gravel shat down from the
holy crapper. Out of nowhere it screeched in. It sheared
trees of their limbs and limbs of their leaves. Late tomatoes were turned to paste, and soup was brewed of
Carnival Aspetuck's already pureed sucker pumpkin
guts. Anything brittle or tender, anything with a flutter
of a pulse, it charged itself upon. The hail made mince
of every petal and sliver and feather and spider, and
anything so precariously sinewed it mowed down and
mashed under cherry-sized chunks. It hailed heavy and
dense and seemingly unendingly. At this time of day on
any day other than today, Luddy Upland might have
once been gandering goose nests on the far shore of
Grunts Pond. Had he been sloshing waist deep through
the browning reeds only strokes from the nests and had
he gotten caught in such an onslaught, he would not
have known whether to cover his head or his mouth as
he witnessed the ice chunks scramble every last sun-
nyside-upper he would have been trying to poach. In
the back yard of her family's outhouse, Zebeliah Was-
She-a-Hackensack-or-Was-She-a-Whiskerhooven might
have been tending her wild bees at 3:33 when all hail

broke loose and no doubt her hives would have done so, too. That pine privy had been the Hackensack-or-Whiskerhooven whocanrememberanymore family's favorite target for spending a box of shells just for the heck of it, and although Zebeliah might have fast took cover in it tucked like an ostrich with her head in the bowl and her ass to high noon those bees would have swooped in through the shot-holes and stung her rump raw. She hadn't the hide Hunko has, and there'd have been no hiding it.

Outside was no place to be out in at 3:33. It was no place for even a ghost to be out in gandering at goose eggs, or in an out-house playing hive-and-seek with yellowjackets lifting your laid-to-rest skirt; or hanging around a clothesline sniffing your sister's spectral up-busters. It was no place to be gathering on True Bliss's rooftop if you were a grackle, and it was without question no place to be pecking about on the ground outside her south-facing parlor oriel if you were a Minton. But there Hunko was, down below a south-facing window, down out of eyeshot of an intimacy too unbearable to swallow: True Bliss serving tea and crackers to Kennesaw Belvedere in the parlor of her house on the anniversary of his birth. It was hailing hard enough to make pterodactyls extinct, but Hunko wasn't evolved enough to care. He was going to put a stop to this repast if it was the last thing he'd ever do.

They'd dig out his bones in another million years and wonder what was up.

Hunko had stormed across the day, across town, across a lifetime up to and under True's south-facing parlor oriel, sure of what was going on in the room he was not tall enough to espy. He had waited a lifetime to be the apple that Kennesaw would bite into and leave True to charm other snakes in other trees, but she had once again tempted him with tea and crackers, and Hunko could stomach it no longer. What likelihood was there that Kennesaw would outlive his ninety-ninth and give Hunko what—a year? a month? a day?—of singular attention; he could not figure a number, it was the idea that counts. After all, he had been so patient. The long stretch of middle years had gone by and he had bid good-bye to everyone he knew but Kennesaw and True, and here was True turning one hundred and Kennesaw ninety-nine and Hunko spry at ninety but there wasn't much time left for patience. True was as wound down as an old clock, ringing off the wrong hours every twenty-seven minutes, and Kennesaw, a minute hand behind her, stuck on five, stuck on nine, stuck on one. It would not be long now before both of them chimed their last off-hour and their wheels slipped their pins and quit spinning. Hunko's lifetime wish seemed so close and so far at the same time: just one day, he wanted—one day—alone with Kennesaw, alone with the beat of his heart, and if it's to be the man's last day, let me be the beat of his. He could not jump high enough to see into True's south-facing parlor oriel but he could see he would have to do more than wait out their assignation if he hoped to get his wish. As the heavens rained down holy hail on him he decided that he would take the parlor by storm and take Kennesaw at last for his own, as Carnival had taken Jubilee.

THERE WERE NOT STONES falling from heaven the day Carnival ran off with his sister in his arms, but the weight of every eye on them came down on them just as smarting. She was moaning all the way from Tumblers' Ridge home, her swollen middle hurt her so. He thought it best to let her rest but she was the one who insisted that if they were going to leave town, let's leave now. He ran in to gather the rucksack she had prepared; she didn't even want to enter the house one last time, so she stayed out on the porch cradling her swell and every now and then eyeing the porch floor beneath her for any telltale proof of trouble, though none came. When Carnival reemerged, he was flushed red to his thick ears with equal parts joy and apprehension—excited to be going but uncertain as to where.

They had no horse nor wagon, no automobile, no tractor, no bicycle, not even a wheelbarrow to get them from here to wherever; all their lives they'd walked New Eden from yonder to home like the felled Drells. But now they would do as no others before them had done, as Kennesaw had almost done but in the end, un-done—they'd be walking from home to yonder for good and all. The tumblers had surely made their ways home by now; the spectators had long since brushed the grass-es out of their hair and smoothed the urgent creases in their overalls; there'd be a pot boiling on someone's cooktop and a candle stub being readied by another's chair; and thusly the solitary nights would continue for the townsfolk who tut-tutted them, the days would fol-low in sameness and the same nights would fall again, but Carnival and Jubilee were setting off for a life no one else would dare live.

It was such a different world from the start. It was dusk when they commenced their trek, still light enough to see the pounded dirt of their main road slip like a lost letter under the thick slab of new macad-am of the road that had forked off their world. In the years since Kennesaw had made this same odyssey, the world beyond New Eden had encroached closer to home. Now here at this junction, hanging as high as the rising moon, they met a red eye blinking in the black that may have been as surprised by them as they were by it; perhaps that's why it was blinking. For a few good minutes, they thought of turning back. They could have gone left, they could have gone right, but left won out, for far that way was a glow of light on the darkening horizon that the cut-through gave glimpse to, while all there was to the right was darkness getting darker and for that they might as well have turned around for home. How small and humbled Carnival felt as they trudged through the cut-through that turned a mountain into air; rock turned to molecules; once mighty, solid, there. Jubilee's slow pace set their pace; more than once, Carnival lifted her in his arms and carried her what must have been miles. Every so often pairs of lights would creep up on them from behind or glare at them from up ahead, and as the lights neared, they slowed at the sight of this burly man and his swollen woman who looked for all the modern world like they were walking out of the past. As each pair of lights sped on and vanished and their walk returned to its dark progress, both brother and sister fought the growing loneliness of night that not even companionship can erase.

There were signs to be seen in the dark but they missed them. The one that would have welcomed them to this neighboring town, and educated them on the familiar differences of its founding and its population, the cluster of enameled medallions alerting them to the many local affiliations of animal orders, the reflective petroglyphs indicative of the activities to be found ahead—eating, excreting, sleeping, wine tasting—and the one with the large letter *H*.

They passed a cluster of houses all identical in shape, all identical in the outlines of light that leached out from the edges of their shaded, shut windows, and not that much farther on, they passed another cluster as identical in its identicals. They passed an odd-looking building of cement as long and low slung as a loaf of bread, with windows too high to see through that had boards nailed over them. A front entry, or what may have served as a front entry, was now an expanse of board as wide as two men, an expanse Carnival himself might have in its former days fit through, had he had it in himself to enter. In front of what looked to be the building's original signage with letters gouged into wood that Carnival could barely decipher beyond an *L* and an *I* and a *B*, was a larger, makeshift sign that crowed a boast beyond Carnival's ken: *Coming Soon: 30,000 Square Feet of New Retail Space*! They passed storefronts blazing with colored lights and fronted in plate glass that shouted out to them the abundance that could be theirs *this week only* at *2 for $29.99, buy 9 get a 10th for half price!* What had been only pairs of lights on the road leading here was now a meteor shower of automotive glitter—flashes of lights and shiny chrome and slick reflective sheens—white lights and red lights and green and amber and orange, some steady, some winking—an eye could not rest on any one light for long. And then there was the din to this town—every surface made a man-made sound, buzzes and hums and rings and clacks and screeches, not only from the vehicles on the roadway but from the doors in the plate-glass facades, metal edges scraping against their metal jambs, and trash can lids flipping—even street corners were chattery with the sounds of invisible mechanical birds chirping.

Back home they were accustomed to forest tracery but here above their heads were only wires and poles and vaguely windmill-ish structures of crisscrossed armatures that reached for the stars. Jubilee convulsed like the red eye earlier, a stitch in her was jabbing the devil's rhythm. In Carnival's arms she was as hot and sweaty as a day's work and the stitch heaved her body inwards from both ends as if her brother was playing her like an accordion. She could not speak through the pain, but the sounds that escaped her through the enveloping din were cries that would draw even a Cro-Magnon from the comfort of his cave. It must be time, Carnival thought, though he could not say these words out loud for fear of his sister's fear. His steps became broader; the muscles that had burst his seams and set in motion the moment now in his arms ached with a new sense of urgency more powerful and more immediate than any he'd ever known. On his back the rucksack juddered and thugged against him, in his arms his sister jostled and flinched and suddenly lay limp; if he hadn't sheathed the ax blade slung over his shoulder, it would have jumped itself right into his skull.

The letter *H* he had not noticed on the sign in the dark was now a sign he could see, blue, with a white arrow on a smaller sign below it, an arrow like the one dweller first drew in his own excrement on the face of a cliff, but an eye could follow this arrow as it pointed away from the street to another sign lit from within, and Carnival's eye scanned across the word etched on that lit-from-within sign, and if ever there was a moment a man could deem an *EMERGENCY*, this was it.

FROM DARKNESS TO ALL that bright white light inside must be what folks mean when they talk about heaven. Carnival had never seen so much bright not made from the day over his head, and unlike outside it was so hushed in there he was almost ashamed to breathe. There was only one person in this bright, noiseless space— seated behind a counter, behind a box on a shelf, a box bathing her in blue, a drowsy-eyed woman of such dark complexion that Carnival was stunned any human could have lasted so long in the sun without turning to ash. A nameplate on her breast said her name was Lak'isha. What an odd name, Carnival thought. The sound of the plate-glass doors disappearing in a hush roused her attention their way, and eyeing the urgent man and his slack woman pivoted her drowse to a stick beside the box and spoke into it and filled the sleepy air around them with a single wake-up word: *Kip!* From behind another pair of hushing doors a boy with a man's face stubble steered a rolling chair their way, locked its wheels, chunked its plates, and plucked Jubilee from Carnival's arms before Carnival could even say his piece; the boy then set Jubilee on the seat and her feet on the plates he unchunked, unlocked the wheels, said over his shoulder to the drowsy-eyed woman behind the counter *bay two*, and with the urgency of a plowman trying to outrun a howler, wheeled Jubilee back through the inside disappearing doors where she disappeared in a hush from Carnival's care and love and lust and fervor forever.

PEOPLE THINK WHAT THEY want to think, but it wasn't what people thought. In a room where Carnival was not, there was to be found in Jubilee a kind of carbuncle in the sac where no carbuncle should grow, born of too much New Eden and not enough world. It was explained to him that Jubilee's swell was seepage and pusses swamping the sac and its surroundings, as the carbuncle in its urgency fed on his sister and grew off of her and pissed out the poisons her own body created with no help from him. In a room where he was not they opened up his sister like she was a damaged parcel and found her contents mangled and spoiled and reeking. The stitch was a burst, a dike undammed that loosed a final toxic pond. He'd known this bucktoothed beauty all his life—she was the urge he could not control; his soul, his closed boast that broke open. He thought he knew her body, thought he knew what was growing in her body, but in her body, her body was growing something else—a strange form her body could not outlive, and that strange form in her made her a stranger to them both. And now that strange form had taken from him not just the one body he finally had but, too, the one he always wanted, leaving him bereft of both the fact of their lives as well as the fiction they thought was real. A man, this time, with a man's face but a boy's body, said there was nothing they could have done—if only he'd brought her here sooner. More words followed but Carnival breathed in loud enough to block out all other sounds. He had heard the one word about his sister that ended his life, and so he did not ever need to hear any others.

CARNIVAL LIVED OUT AS many years beyond burying his sister as he could stand. He had stopped his ax from swinging, which stopped his muscles from swelling, which stopped his seams from bursting, but that did not stop his urges from coming. Day followed same day and night after same night he sat his deflating self in Jubilee's mending chair in the corner of their house between the window and the woodstove and he fondled her bobbins and he tongued her threads, and oh, how he wished he were feeding into her needle's eye. The repetition night after same night swelled him to the edge of bursting, but he kept himself stored up; he would not let his feelings spill, not for all the rest of his years, not a single drop—not on his sister's heck box, and not on her memory. A man can do without only so long, however, before he decides there is no reason to do without any longer, or so it may be that his body decides this for him, for Carnival's body seemed to swell up with the same strange swell that swelled his sister to bursting, although the poisons that pissed him cold were all on account of her.

And this is how he would remain. In the unearthed box where Hunko placed Carnival's body encoiled with the remnants of Jubilee's, just as their father's body had been placed with their mother's before them, the brother's every uncontainable urge for his sister was entombed in its swollen state for eternity.

HUNKO WOULD CRY with like-mindedness thinking back on it if he thought he had enough time. What Carnival had lived beyond and lived without, Hunko could not bear another minute of himself. Inside was

Kennesaw and the how-many-more-minutes of life Hunko might have with him, and inside, too, was True, and she was anything but a blissful impediment. He stomped his muddy boots on her front steps and he mudded her porch floor just as much, and he shoved open her already ajar front vestibule door like it was a cape and he was a bull and the door hit the wall and the glass in it smashed into a million pretty shards of un-pent resentment, and he mudded into her entry with the intent of mudding his way in between them once and for all, only once inside, he was struck dumb in his boots like a mastodon suddenly dropped in tar.

First, there was the stench. It wasn't from him; he checked. Then there was the clutter, not what he expect-ed from True; that made him smile. And he was sur-prised to see no tea, no saltines, no sign of celebration at all in the front parlor at first glance, so he stepped with caution into the dining room and was on his way through the debris into the kitchen when down among the debris beside the table there was True—on the floor and on her side; and from the ease of her old flesh on her old face he didn't even need to feel her skin, from that look of her alone he knew, like every old man knows—she was on her way.

A younger man might have cried out and hurled himself hydroelectrically to make her millpond stir, but Hunko knew when calm honored calm. He knelt to her and held her hard gnarled hand in his and felt the cool of it, and touched her brow with his nubby palm and felt the cool there, too, and there was no more need to dip a toe in those waters—he had his answer, and that answer gave him peace. The end fills in an empty space like a rush of ocean and it does not matter if you witness the very moment it flows in or not—it comes; and against its force you hold what you can and you let the flow take what it must, and the feelings you may have held back for those things the flood washes away, you must let wash away with those things or you, too, will drown; and Hunko found his own tide of jealousy flowing away with the waters that carried True, and he was there on the shore waving her farewell and wishing her his most sincere good wishes that she have herself a pleasant journey. True Bliss did not reach the day that would make her a century, but Hunko figured she was part of a continuum that started the day the first green sprout lifted its head to the sky, and that made her older than one hundred years; that made her ageless. He did not have enough in him to build her a box or dig her a hole or even take her to her bed. He laid her hand down closer to her heart and patted her shoulder and stood his old self up and wiped his sniffer with the back of his hand and nodded his head at her and smiled and said, *Old girl, good-bye.*

Where he did churn was now in his concern for Kennesaw—where was he? *Kennesaw? Ken-ne-saw!* He wasn't in the dining room, and not in the kitchen behind it, and though he heard a rattle he saw the rattle a split second later, a raccoon—*git!* He then dodged more debris on his way to the front hallway and into the squalor of the parlor and there behind a stack of wooden apple crates where he had not fully looked before, face down on the filthy rug, was the most glorious cleft and chisel that had ever graced the earth—his Kennesaw. *Ken-ne-saw!*

Calm might honor calm when calm is all that comes but Kennesaw stirred and that sent Hunko hydraulic. He was on his old knees by Kennesaw's side as fast as a tree can fall and turning Kennesaw over with as much care and reverence as one would turn a page of the Good Book. When he cradled Kennesaw's head in his nubby hands and Kennesaw's bluer-than-blues fluttered Hunko into their field of vision, and the fear in them eased to peace, and he smiled up at that Minton sniffer above, you'd swear it was a tableau of a mother and her brand new child at the moment they knew they were at the beginning of the rest of their lives.

Hunko helped Kennesaw to his feet and sat him back down on the davenport from which he had sprung. There was a sheen of pee on Kennesaw's chisel from where his face had planted in the puddle on the rug, and slipping down his cleft a dribble of blood from where his lip split a bit, and in the crack and crotch of his pants was a dark spot too dark to be old. Hunko smoothed the hair off Kennesaw's brow and held his handsome old face in his nubby hand and it occurred to Hunko that in all his life he had never stood taller than Kennesaw until this very moment, and how he had kept himself a boy yearning for Kennesaw all these years until this moment when he was now needed as a man.

He took a rag from the davenport and went to the kitchen to wet it so he could clean his friend's face of the indignity of his day. The raccoon he had shooed not too long ago had claimed the sinktop for his own, but jumped from it to an open drawer nearby when Hunko stepped within hissing distance. Hunko wanted that rag to be as cool and soothing on Kennesaw's face as the waters of Galilee, and he pumped that pump with all the might in him to dredge from the bottom of time as much cold cleansing comfort as that dirty old rag could soak in. And as he dug for his something so deep down, so, too, did the raccoon in the drawer dig for who-knows-what, both of them sharing a determination to find that special something the eye cannot readily see. Hunko finished his pumping and wrung out the rag and snapped it at the raccoon and the raccoon lumbered for cover inside the cookstove, and with him out of the way Hunko peered into the drawer to see what all that pawing was about, but nothing in there seemed to him worth a raccoon's trouble. It was a drawer full of pennies and pins: a hammer head missing its handle, a spoon in the bend of a hook, an apple core dried to a fossil, scraps of burlap and squiggles of twine and a frayed cut end of pale pink velvet, and generations of assorted miscellany and other nonsense from lives as everyday as this 'n' that. Here, too, was True no more towering than he was in her lone going; in the end she was just as much a sentimental slob as anybody else.

Hunko never cleaned anything as clean as he cleaned Kennesaw. The cool water was worth every bit of his effort for it returned to the man's face the hue of the still living. *True's gone*, Hunko told him then, and Kennesaw looked up at Hunko with bluer-than-blues that took on only the slimmest glimmer of slick, for there was not much liquid left in the man and whatever there was he needed to shed only for himself. He cupped Hunko's nubby hand, the one so gently cooling his face with the rag, the hand that no matter how much of a man Hunko was right now was still smaller than his own, and he stopped Hunko's hand from its gentle business, and with his hand there on Hunko's, said to Hunko the three tenderest words Hunko had ever wanted to hear in his life; he said to Hunko, *Take me home.*

THERE IS THE SHORE we see from the distance when we are young and we think we are the first to see it and we are the only ones to know it is there, yet as we near it closer and closer it gives way to a shore more distant that is the real shore we are born to want to reach. It is the shore that made the first dweller leave the comfort of his cave, and his cousin the spear wielder find in the air a reason to do more than just live; it is the far shore that drew to this spot, this New Eden, the men and women who made what they could of the time they had here, and who traveled from here to an even more distant shore that no one will be left to recall.

The day's weather had soothed from its fevered state to almost sleepy, but the day was getting late and Kennesaw did not have the strength in him to make the long walk home, even if he leaned on Hunko all the way. They walked along the long untraveled dirt that had once defined the center of their own pocket of paradise, and past Nedewen Field and its mouth full of old teeth that in time would wear to nubs of nothing, and beyond there as the moon began to rise through Saflutises' gone-to-seed fields and past the rubble of Buckett barns and the fallen down structures of families long ago fallen from memory, and through to the thinning thick of woods that led from the clearing where the Drells' wanderings ended. The morning's stop-up in Kennesaw was starting to un-stop and he was growing too unstable to go beyond to Tumblers' Ridge or the ridge beyond that that was spooked by the memory of Mawz, or make it all the way back to his own house where he might pass through Hunko's gates for one last time, or make it out to Hunko's place where Hunko had kept his matching pair of gates in swinging order should Kennesaw ever come to call; so they stopped for however long they'd need to rest on the shores of Grunts Pond, and Hunko helped Kennesaw sit his tired old self down on the rock of their remembered youth, and sat himself down right next to him close, and breathed in the balsam air like a very first breath and said to Kennesaw *happy birthday*, and Kennesaw smiled and said back *yes, it is*; then Kennesaw laid an arm around Hunko's humped shoulder and it fit just right, and these two old men sat that way for as long as we can tell until their moon went down in the sky.

AUTHOR BIO

ROBERT HILL is a New Englander by birth, a West Coaster by choice, and an Oregonian by osmosis. As a writer, he has worked in advertising, entertainment, educational software, and not-for-profit fundraising. He is a recipient of a Literary Arts Walt Morey Fellowship and a Bread Loaf Writers' Conference Fellowship. His debut novel, *When All Is Said and Done* (Graywolf Press), was shortlisted for the Oregon Book Awards' Ken Kesey Award for Fiction.

ACKNOWLEDGMENTS

THE AUTHOR would like to thank the following people whose encouragement and support, from early on to completion and beyond, made the writing of this novel possible: Tom Spanbauer and the Dangerous Writers, Steve Arndt, Elizabeth Scott, Kathleen Lane, Dian Greenwood, and John Parker. Thank you to Gigi Little for bringing art out of the earth. Thanks to Mary Bisbee-Beek for her amazing publicity smarts, stamina, and enthusiasm. Thanks most of all to the ferociously talented Laura Stanfill, without whom this book simply would not be.

READERS' GUIDE

1. Is *The Remnants* a love story? Why or why not?

2. What kind of a book would *The Remnants* be if it had been written without whimsy? What other authors reach deep into difficult subjects through humor and wit? How would your reaction to the book change if the characters had more normal names?

3. This novel is about aging and the final days of a community, but the word "death" never appears, and "die" appears only once. Can you find it?

4. Are there main characters in this novel? If so, who are they, and how does Robert Hill emphasize them over the others? If not, list some of the characters who have big roles in shaping New Eden's trajectory.

5. Who is the narrator? Is it one person? Is it a person at all?

6. Name some factors that contribute to New Eden's decline. Would any one thing have stopped, or slowed, its end?

7. Why does Kennesaw leave to study at the library? Why does he come back home every night?

8. True Bliss takes on a leadership role in New Eden. Name one or more instances where she alters the course of the town.

9. What is the purpose of folding so many memories into what is essentially a single story? How do the memories add weight to the front story tea-party plot?

10. Is the cover a graveyard? A path? Stone tablets?

11. New Eden is not anchored by real-world geography. Where do you think it is? Have you visited any ghost towns or once-thriving communities that now have small or nonexistent populations? Why do you think the author made the choice to avoid setting it in a "real" place?

12. Talk about dweller. Why is he part of the book? Does his presence make the fate of this particular town more universal? How about spear-wielder?

13. Each chapter of *The Remnants* could be considered a short story. Why did the author choose to use this format to write about the fate of a small town? Why do you think this book is labeled as a novel instead of a linked story collection? Are there any chapters that don't work as independent pieces?

14. This novel features numerous riffs on the indignities of aging. How is True's aging shown? Kennesaw's? Hunko's?

15. Would you want to live in such an isolated town? Why or why not?

To invite Robert Hill to your book club, contact him through forestavenuepress.com or roberthill-theremnants.com.